Sir Arthur Conan Doyle's
The Adventure of the Empty House

Adapted by: Vincent Goodwin

Illustrated by: Ben Dunn

magic
wagon

visit us at
www.abdopublishing.com

Published by Magic Wagon, a division of the ABDO Group, 8000 West 78th Street, Edina, Minnesota, 55439. Copyright © 2010 by Abdo Consulting Group, Inc. International copyrights reserved in all countries. All rights reserved. No part of this book may be reproduced in any form without written permission from the publisher.

Graphic Planet™ is a trademark and logo of Magic Wagon.

Printed in the United States of America, North Mankato, Minnesota.
102009
012010

 PRINTED ON RECYCLED PAPER

Original novel by Sir Arthur Conan Doyle
Adapted by Vincent Goodwin
Illustrated by Ben Dunn
Colored by Robby Bevard & GURU-eFX
Edited by Stephanie Hedlund and Rochelle Baltzer
Interior layout and design by Antarctic Press
Cover art by Ben Dunn
Cover design by Abbey Fitzgerald

Library of Congress Cataloging-in-Publication Data

Goodwin, Vincent.
 The Adventure of the Empty House / written by Sir Arthur Conan Doyle ; adapted by Vincent Goodwin ; illustrated by Ben Dunn.
 p. cm. -- (The graphic novel adventures of Sherlock Holmes)
 Summary: Retells in graphic novel format a story featuring the great English detective Sherlock Holmes.
 Includes bibliographical references.
 ISBN 978-1-60270-724-5
 1. Graphic novels. [1. Graphic novels. 2. Doyle, Arthur Conan, Sir, 1859-1930. Adventure of the Empty House—Adaptations. 3. Mystery and detective stories.] I. Dunn, Ben, ill. II. Doyle, Arthur Conan, Sir, 1859-1930. Adventure of the Empty House. III. Title. IV. Title.

PZ7.7.G66Ad 2010
741.5'973--dc22

                                                                2009032458

Table of Contents

Cast

Sherlock Holmes

Dr. John Watson

Colonel Sebastian Moran

Inspector Lestrade

Professor Moriarty

Ronald Adair

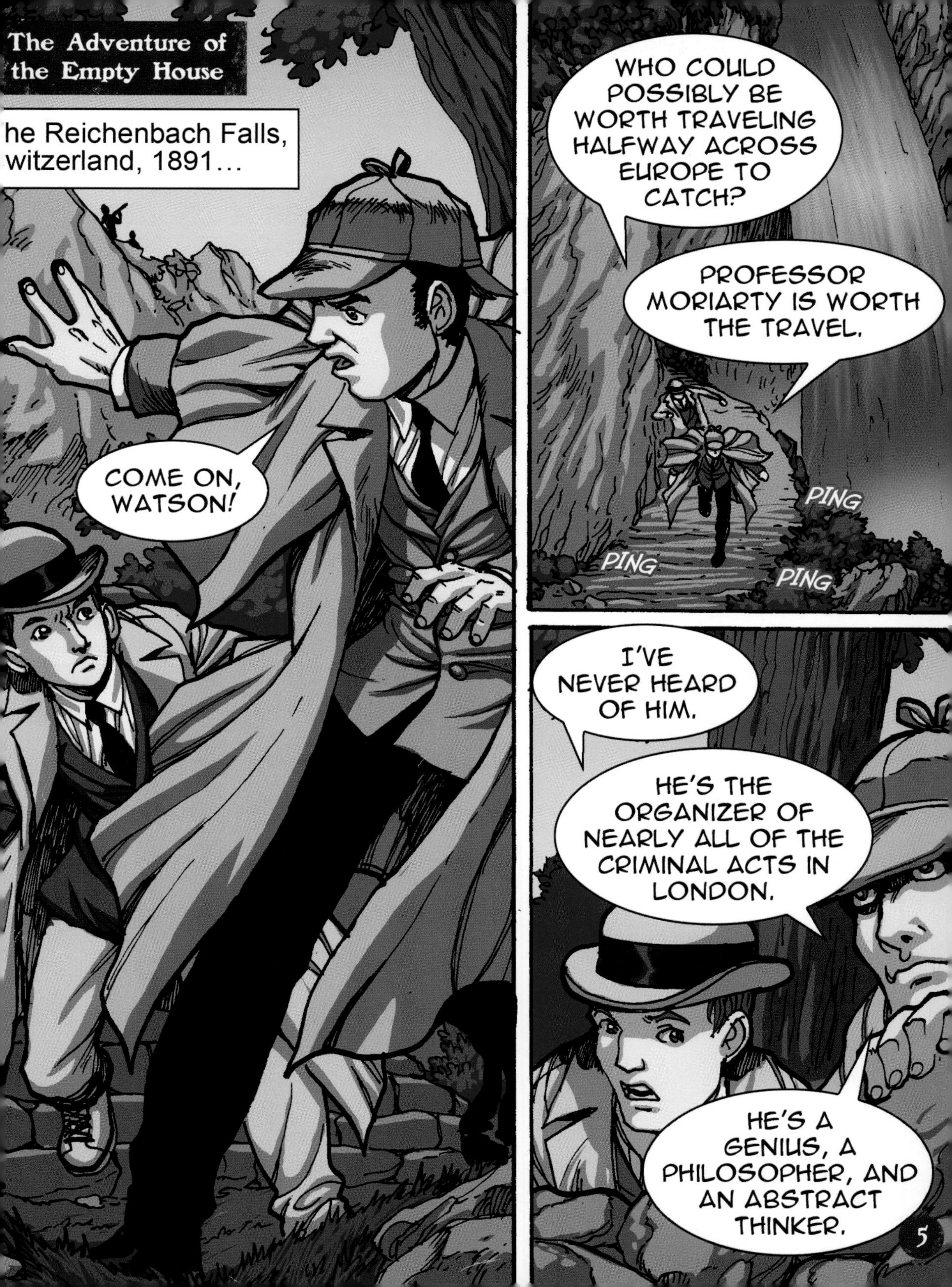
The Adventure of the Empty House
he Reichenbach Falls, witzerland, 1891…
COME ON, WATSON!
WHO COULD POSSIBLY BE WORTH TRAVELING HALFWAY ACROSS EUROPE TO CATCH?
PROFESSOR MORIARTY IS WORTH THE TRAVEL.
PING
PING
PING
I'VE NEVER HEARD OF HIM.
HE'S THE ORGANIZER OF NEARLY ALL OF THE CRIMINAL ACTS IN LONDON.
HE'S A GENIUS, A PHILOSOPHER, AND AN ABSTRACT THINKER.

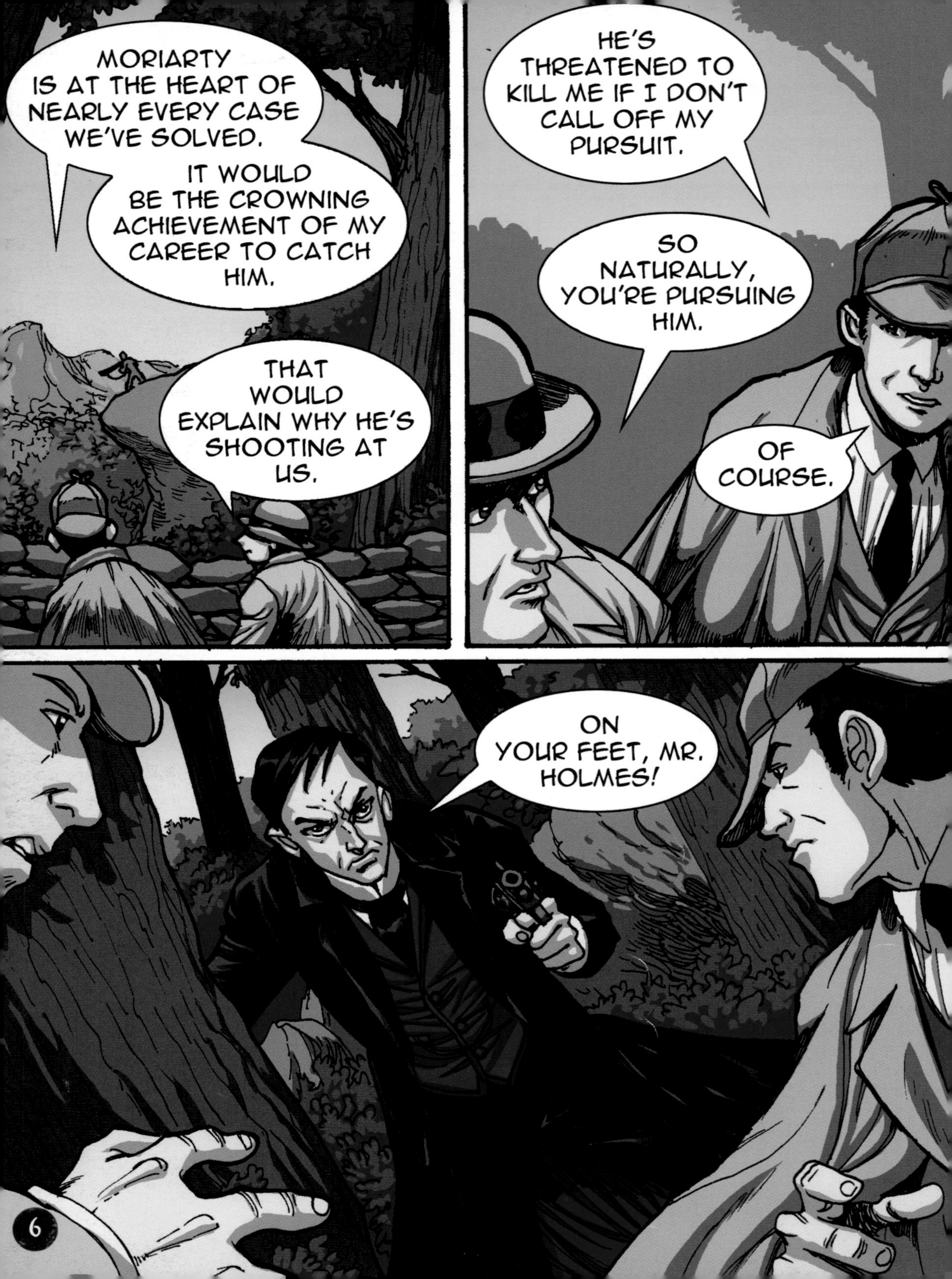
MORIARTY IS AT THE HEART OF NEARLY EVERY CASE WE'VE SOLVED.
IT WOULD BE THE CROWNING ACHIEVEMENT OF MY CAREER TO CATCH HIM.
THAT WOULD EXPLAIN WHY HE'S SHOOTING AT US.
HE'S THREATENED TO KILL ME IF I DON'T CALL OFF MY PURSUIT.
SO NATURALLY, YOU'RE PURSUING HIM.
OF COURSE.
ON YOUR FEET, MR. HOLMES!

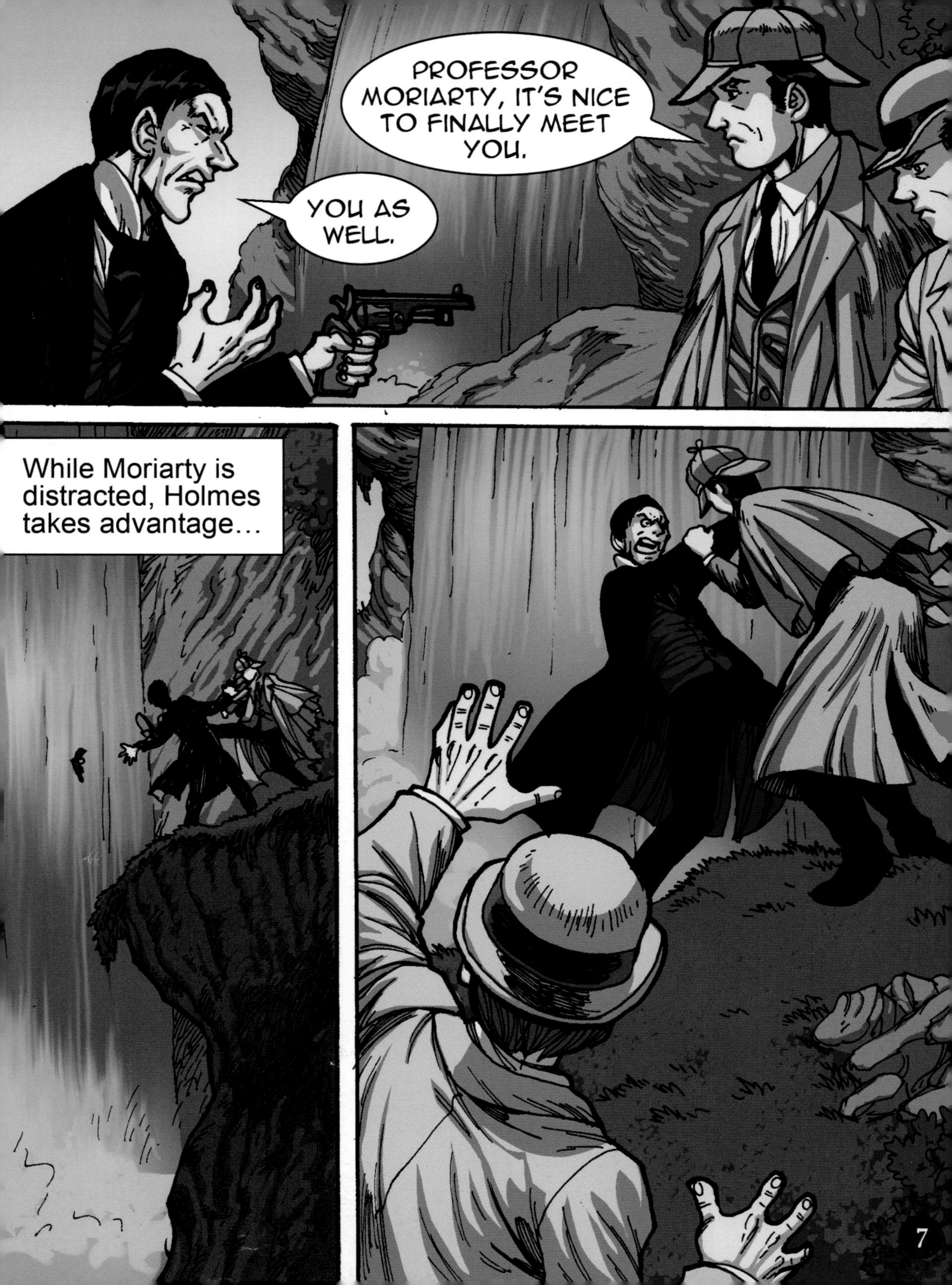
PROFESSOR MORIARTY, IT'S NICE TO FINALLY MEET YOU.
YOU AS WELL.
While Moriarty is distracted, Holmes takes advantage…

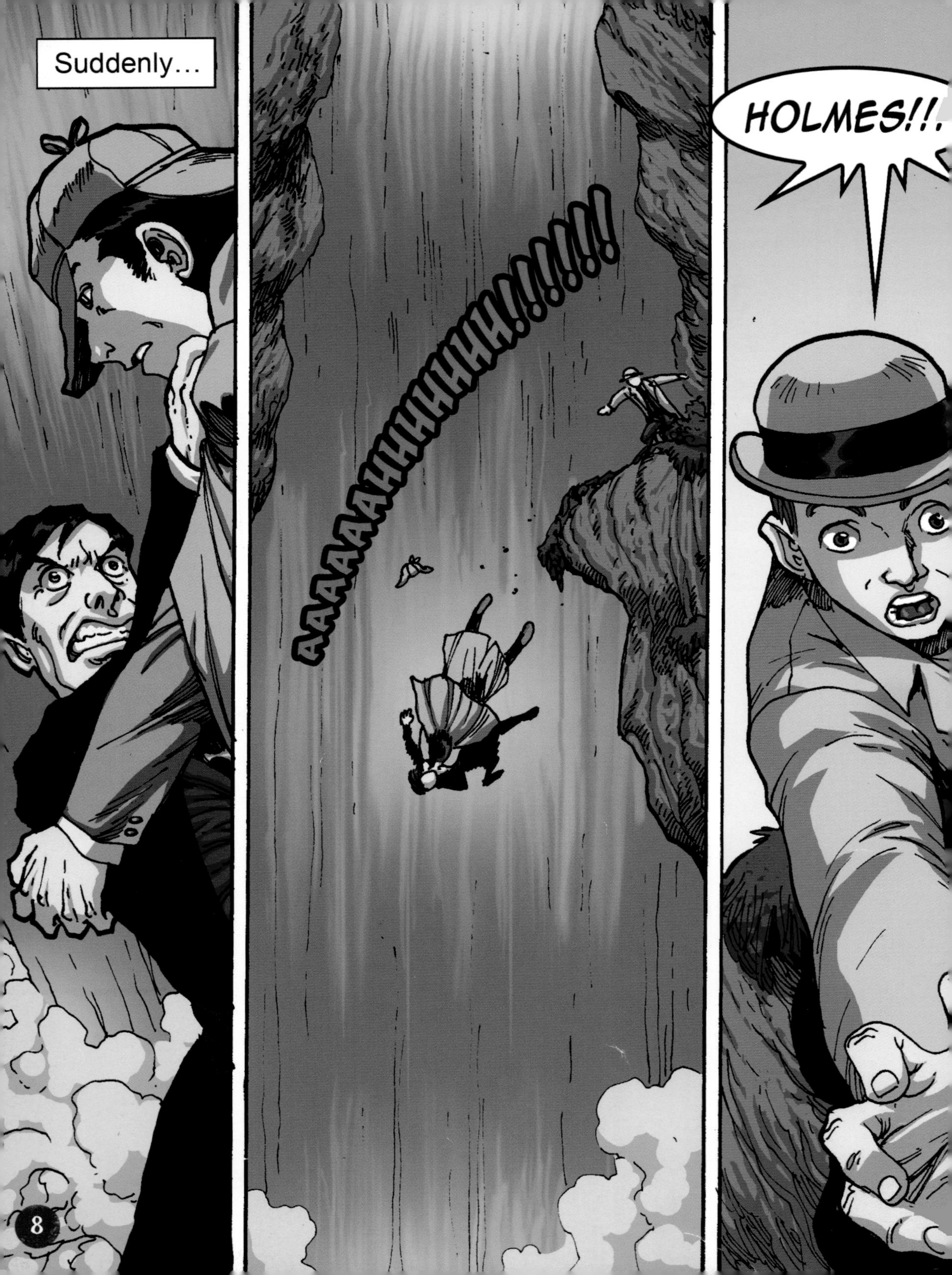
Suddenly...
AAAAAAHHHHHHH!!!!!!
HOLMES!!.

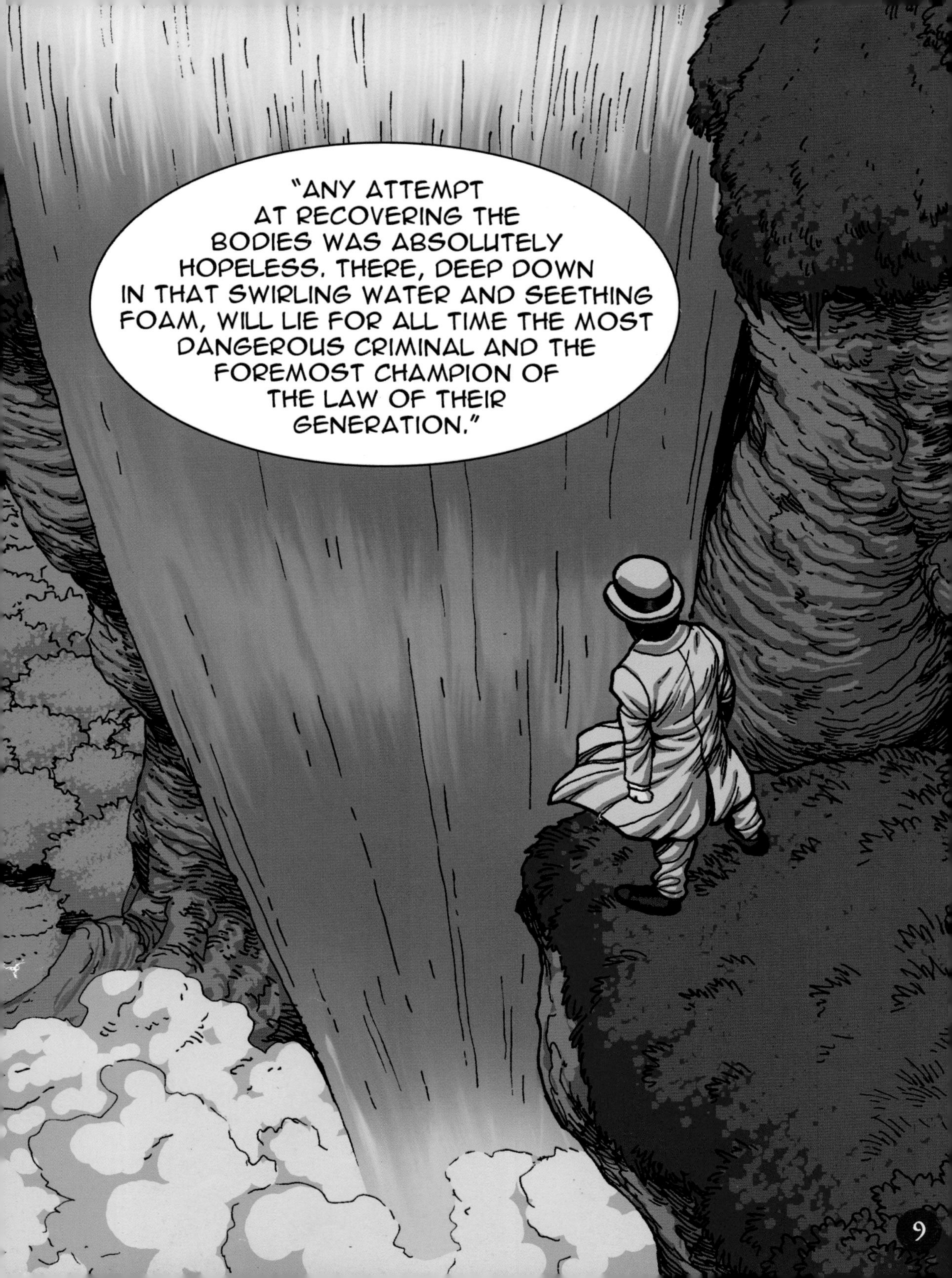
"ANY ATTEMPT AT RECOVERING THE BODIES WAS ABSOLUTELY HOPELESS. THERE, DEEP DOWN IN THAT SWIRLING WATER AND SEETHING FOAM, WILL LIE FOR ALL TIME THE MOST DANGEROUS CRIMINAL AND THE FOREMOST CHAMPION OF THE LAW OF THEIR GENERATION."

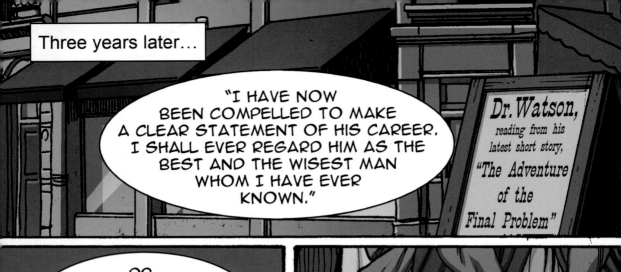

"I HAVE NOW BEEN COMPELLED TO MAKE A CLEAR STATEMENT OF HIS CAREER. I SHALL EVER REGARD HIM AS THE BEST AND THE WISEST MAN WHOM I HAVE EVER KNOWN."

Dr. Watson, reading from his latest short story, "The Adventure of the Final Problem"

DR. WATSON WILL BE SIGNING COPIES OF HIS STORY AT THAT TABLE OVER THERE.

MEMOIRS of SHERLOCK HOLMES

DR. WATSON, IS SHERLOCK HOLMES REALLY GONE?

YES, I AM AFRAID SO. AND THE WORLD IS MUCH THE WORSE FOR IT.

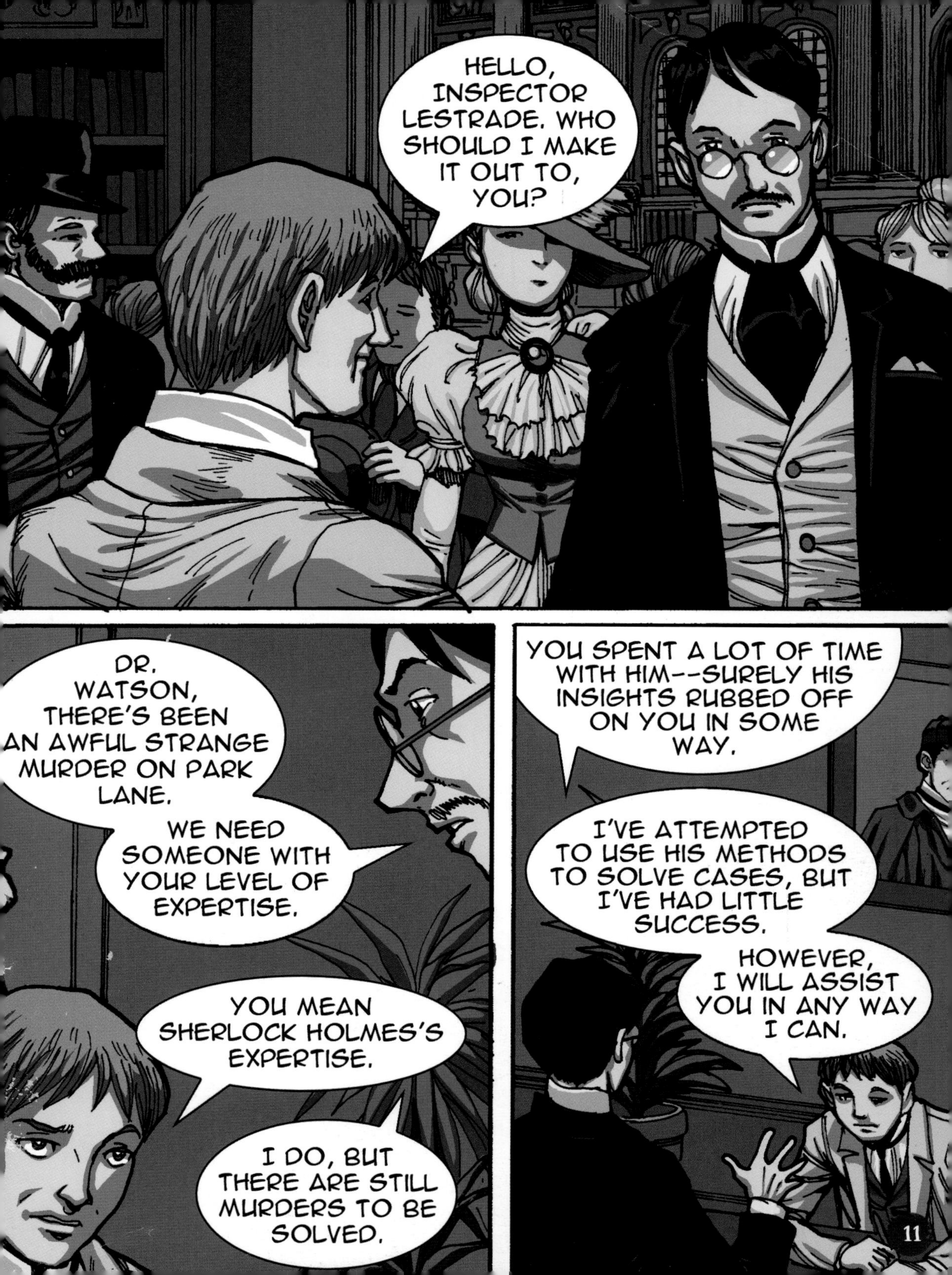
HELLO, INSPECTOR LESTRADE. WHO SHOULD I MAKE IT OUT TO, YOU?
DR. WATSON, THERE'S BEEN AN AWFUL STRANGE MURDER ON PARK LANE.
WE NEED SOMEONE WITH YOUR LEVEL OF EXPERTISE.
YOU MEAN SHERLOCK HOLMES'S EXPERTISE.
I DO, BUT THERE ARE STILL MURDERS TO BE SOLVED.
YOU SPENT A LOT OF TIME WITH HIM--SURELY HIS INSIGHTS RUBBED OFF ON YOU IN SOME WAY.
I'VE ATTEMPTED TO USE HIS METHODS TO SOLVE CASES, BUT I'VE HAD LITTLE SUCCESS.
HOWEVER, I WILL ASSIST YOU IN ANY WAY I CAN.

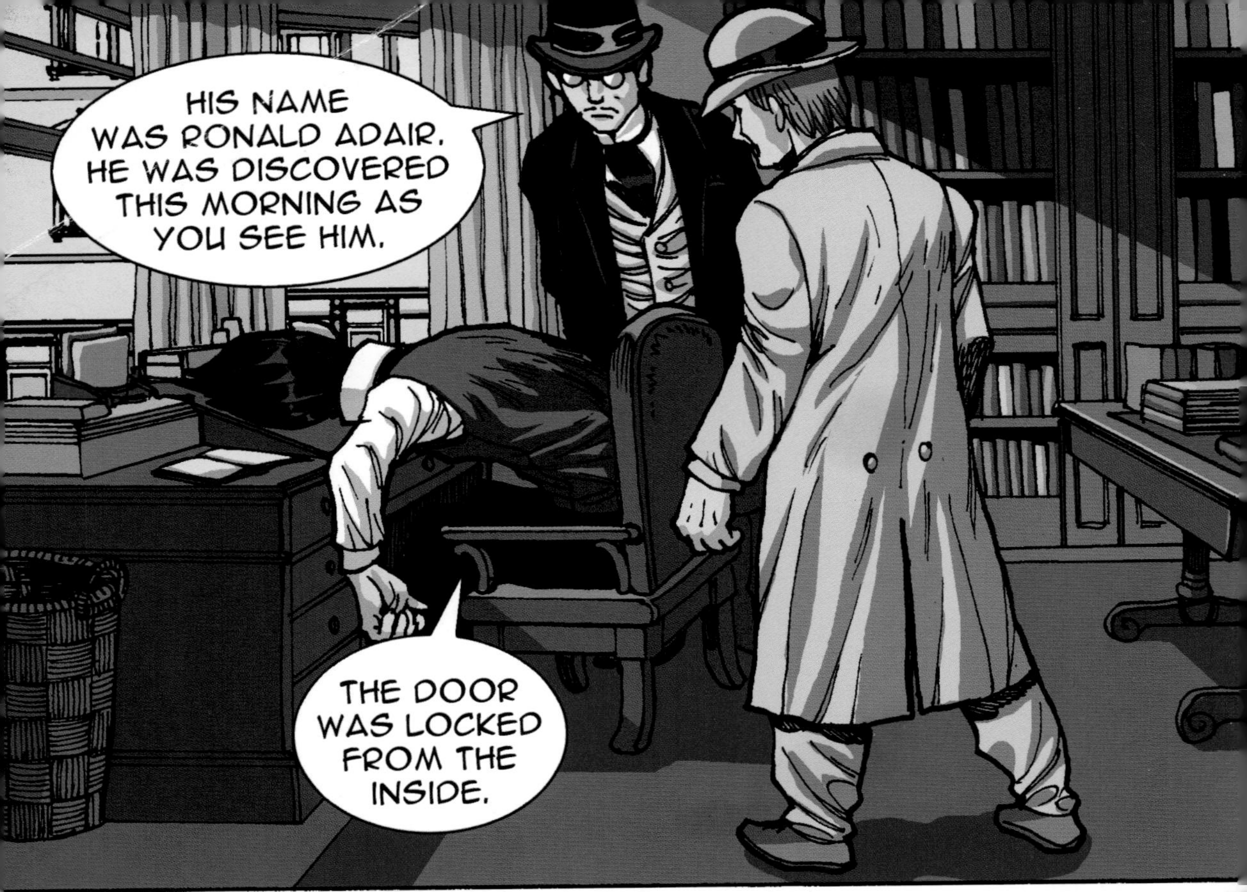
HIS NAME WAS RONALD ADAIR. HE WAS DISCOVERED THIS MORNING AS YOU SEE HIM.
THE DOOR WAS LOCKED FROM THE INSIDE.

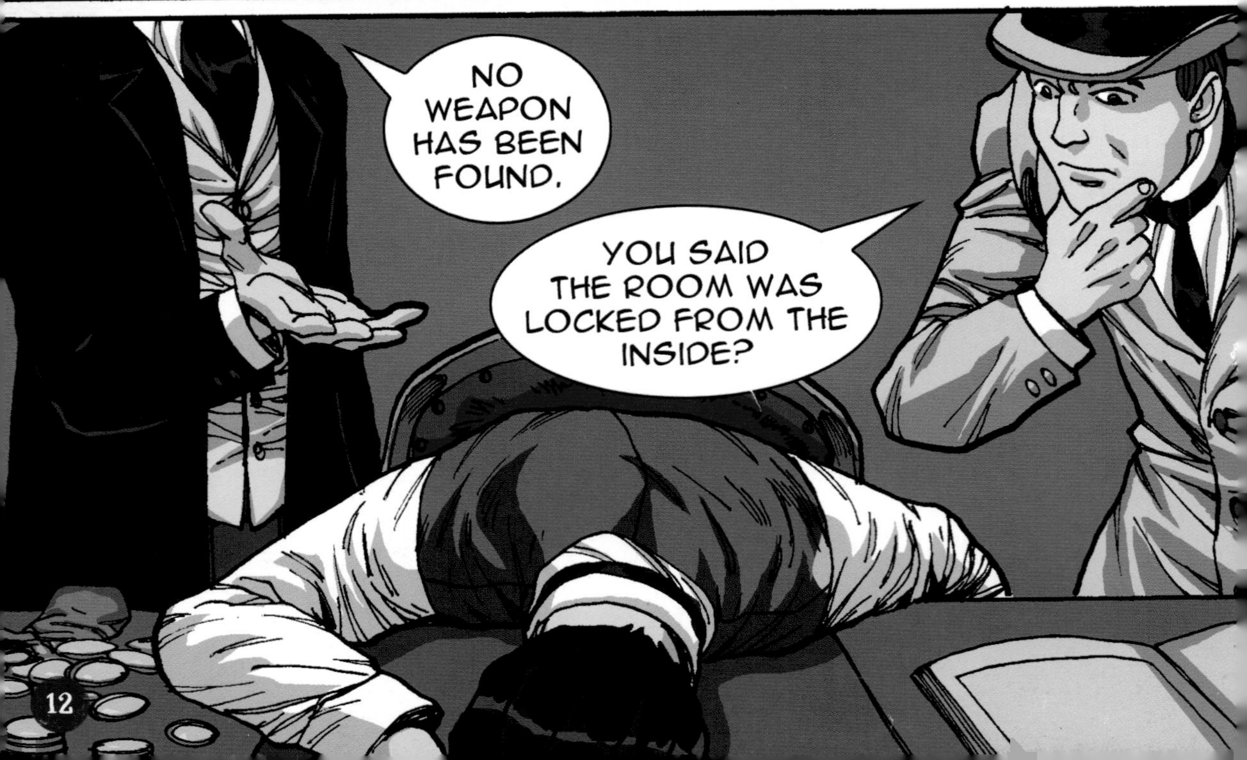
NO WEAPON HAS BEEN FOUND.
YOU SAID THE ROOM WAS LOCKED FROM THE INSIDE?

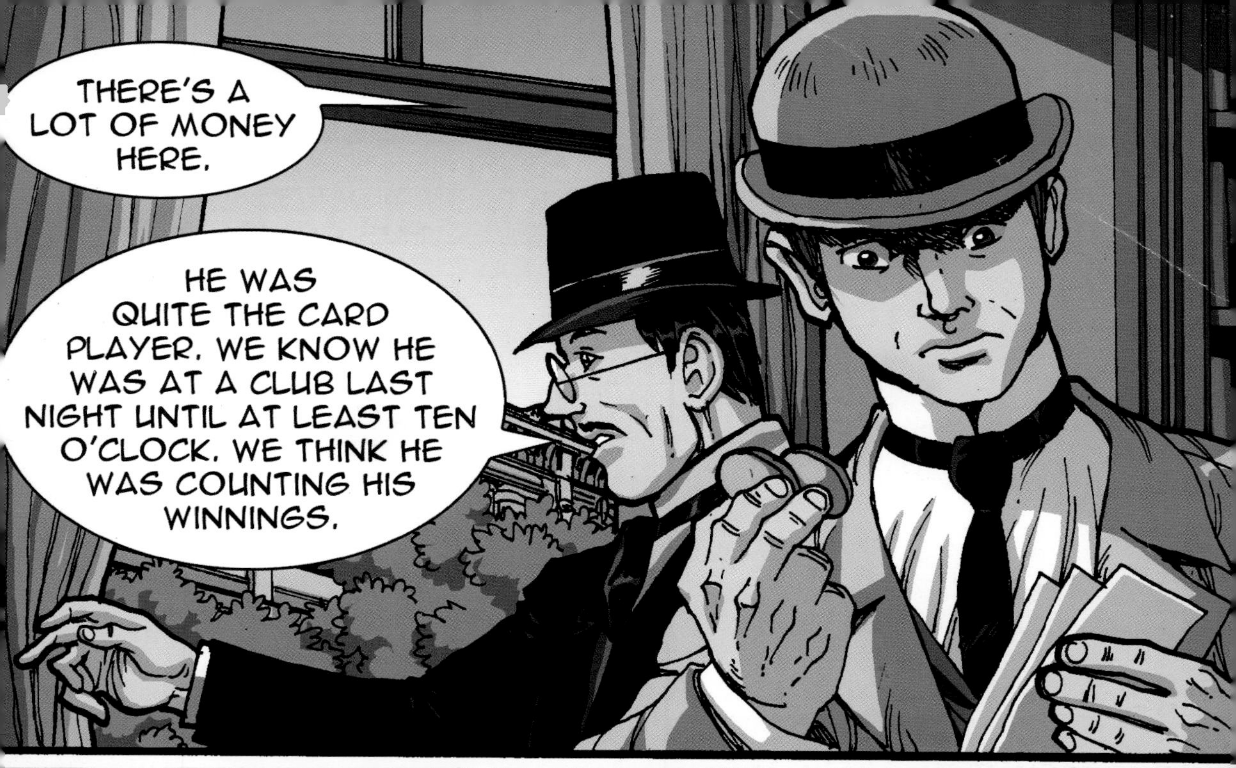
THERE'S A LOT OF MONEY HERE.
HE WAS QUITE THE CARD PLAYER. WE KNOW HE WAS AT A CLUB LAST NIGHT UNTIL AT LEAST TEN O'CLOCK. WE THINK HE WAS COUNTING HIS WINNINGS.

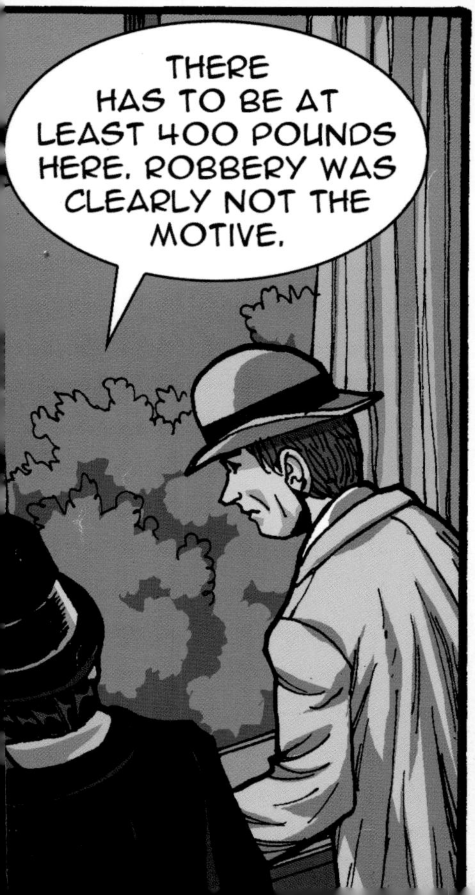
THERE HAS TO BE AT LEAST 400 POUNDS HERE. ROBBERY WAS CLEARLY NOT THE MOTIVE.

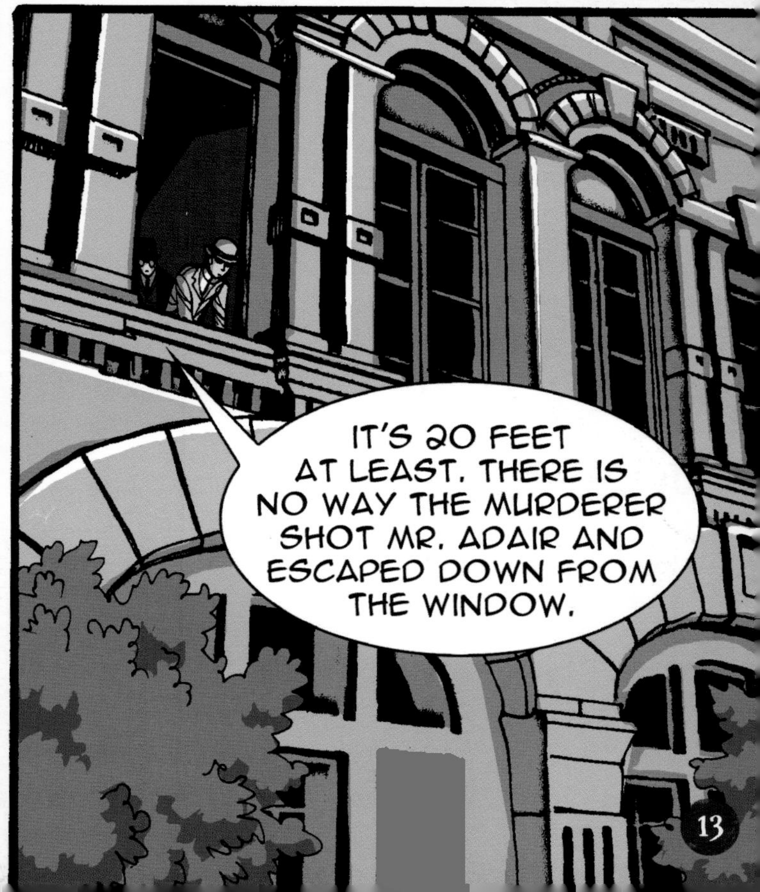
IT'S 20 FEET AT LEAST. THERE IS NO WAY THE MURDERER SHOT MR. ADAIR AND ESCAPED DOWN FROM THE WINDOW.

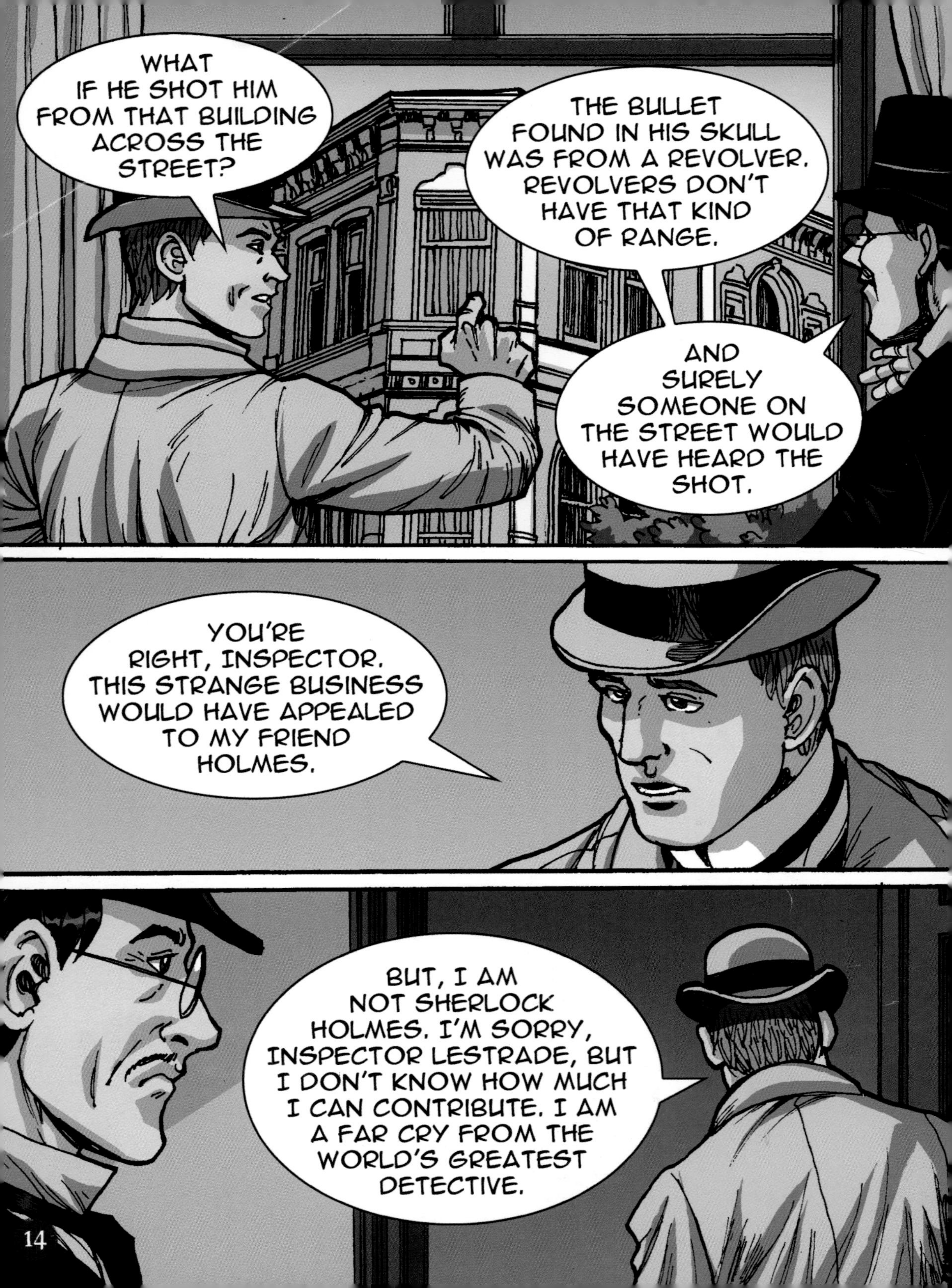
WHAT IF HE SHOT HIM FROM THAT BUILDING ACROSS THE STREET?
THE BULLET FOUND IN HIS SKULL WAS FROM A REVOLVER. REVOLVERS DON'T HAVE THAT KIND OF RANGE.
AND SURELY SOMEONE ON THE STREET WOULD HAVE HEARD THE SHOT.
YOU'RE RIGHT, INSPECTOR. THIS STRANGE BUSINESS WOULD HAVE APPEALED TO MY FRIEND HOLMES.
BUT, I AM NOT SHERLOCK HOLMES. I'M SORRY, INSPECTOR LESTRADE, BUT I DON'T KNOW HOW MUCH I CAN CONTRIBUTE. I AM A FAR CRY FROM THE WORLD'S GREATEST DETECTIVE.

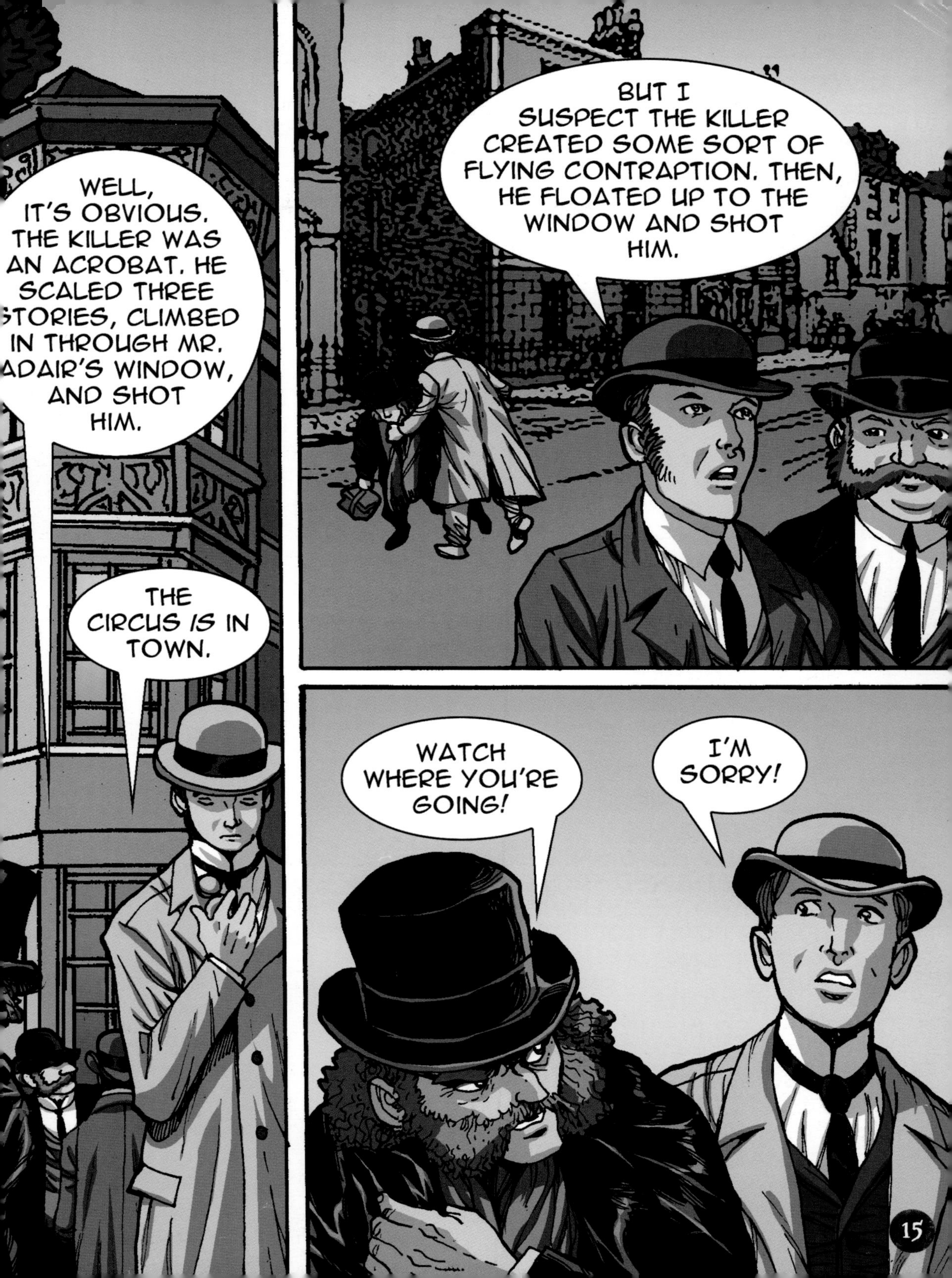
WELL, IT'S OBVIOUS. THE KILLER WAS AN ACROBAT. HE SCALED THREE STORIES, CLIMBED IN THROUGH MR. ADAIR'S WINDOW, AND SHOT HIM.
THE CIRCUS *IS* IN TOWN.
BUT I SUSPECT THE KILLER CREATED SOME SORT OF FLYING CONTRAPTION. THEN, HE FLOATED UP TO THE WINDOW AND SHOT HIM.
WATCH WHERE YOU'RE GOING!
I'M SORRY!

At Watson's home later that night…

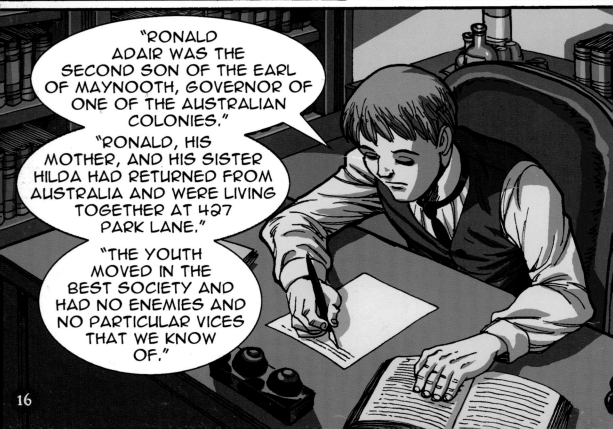

"RONALD ADAIR WAS THE SECOND SON OF THE EARL OF MAYNOOTH, GOVERNOR OF ONE OF THE AUSTRALIAN COLONIES."

"RONALD, HIS MOTHER, AND HIS SISTER HILDA HAD RETURNED FROM AUSTRALIA AND WERE LIVING TOGETHER AT 427 PARK LANE."

"THE YOUTH MOVED IN THE BEST SOCIETY AND HAD NO ENEMIES AND NO PARTICULAR VICES THAT WE KNOW OF."

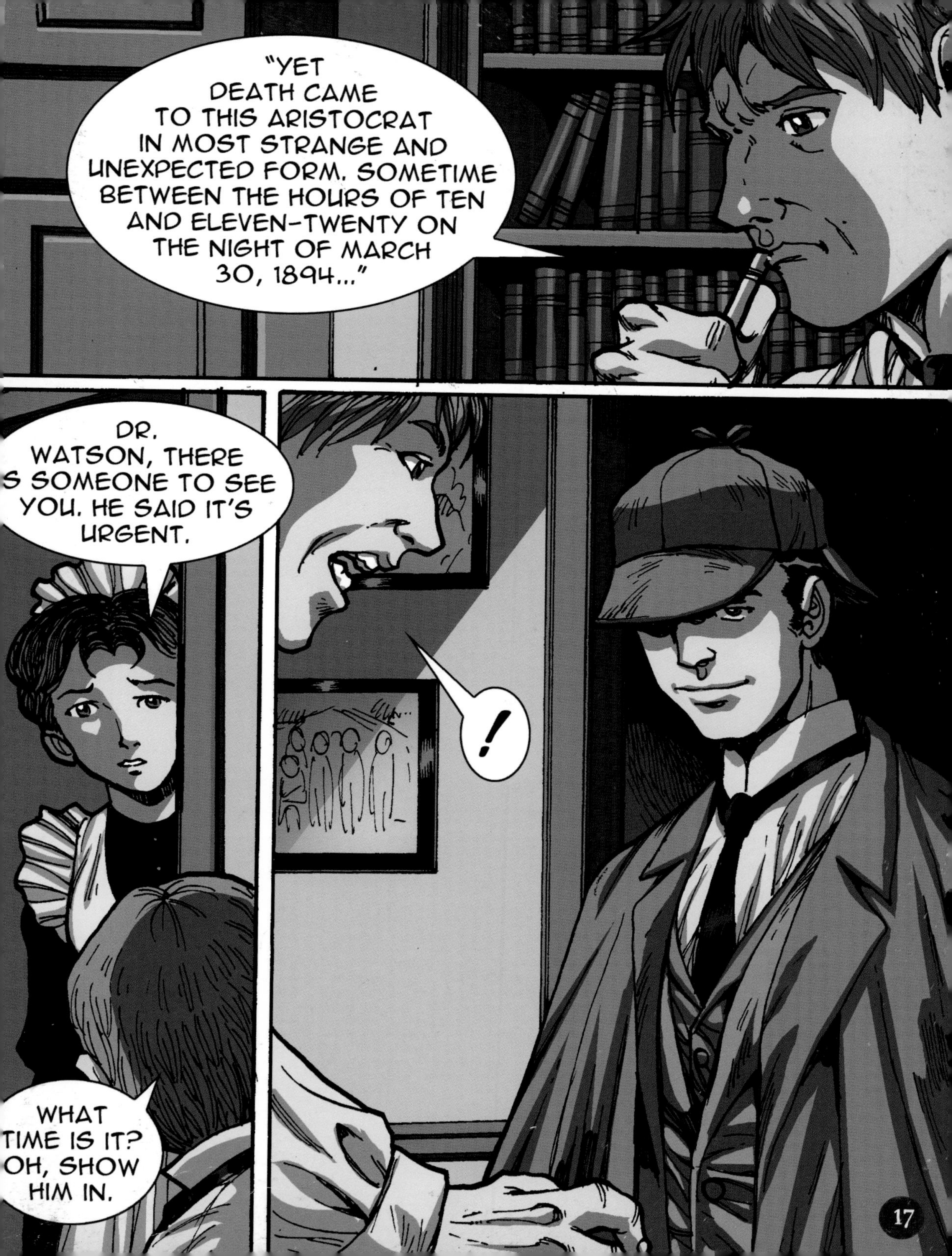
"YET DEATH CAME TO THIS ARISTOCRAT IN MOST STRANGE AND UNEXPECTED FORM. SOMETIME BETWEEN THE HOURS OF TEN AND ELEVEN-TWENTY ON THE NIGHT OF MARCH 30, 1894..."
DR. WATSON, THERE S SOMEONE TO SEE YOU. HE SAID IT'S URGENT.
!
WHAT TIME IS IT? OH, SHOW HIM IN.

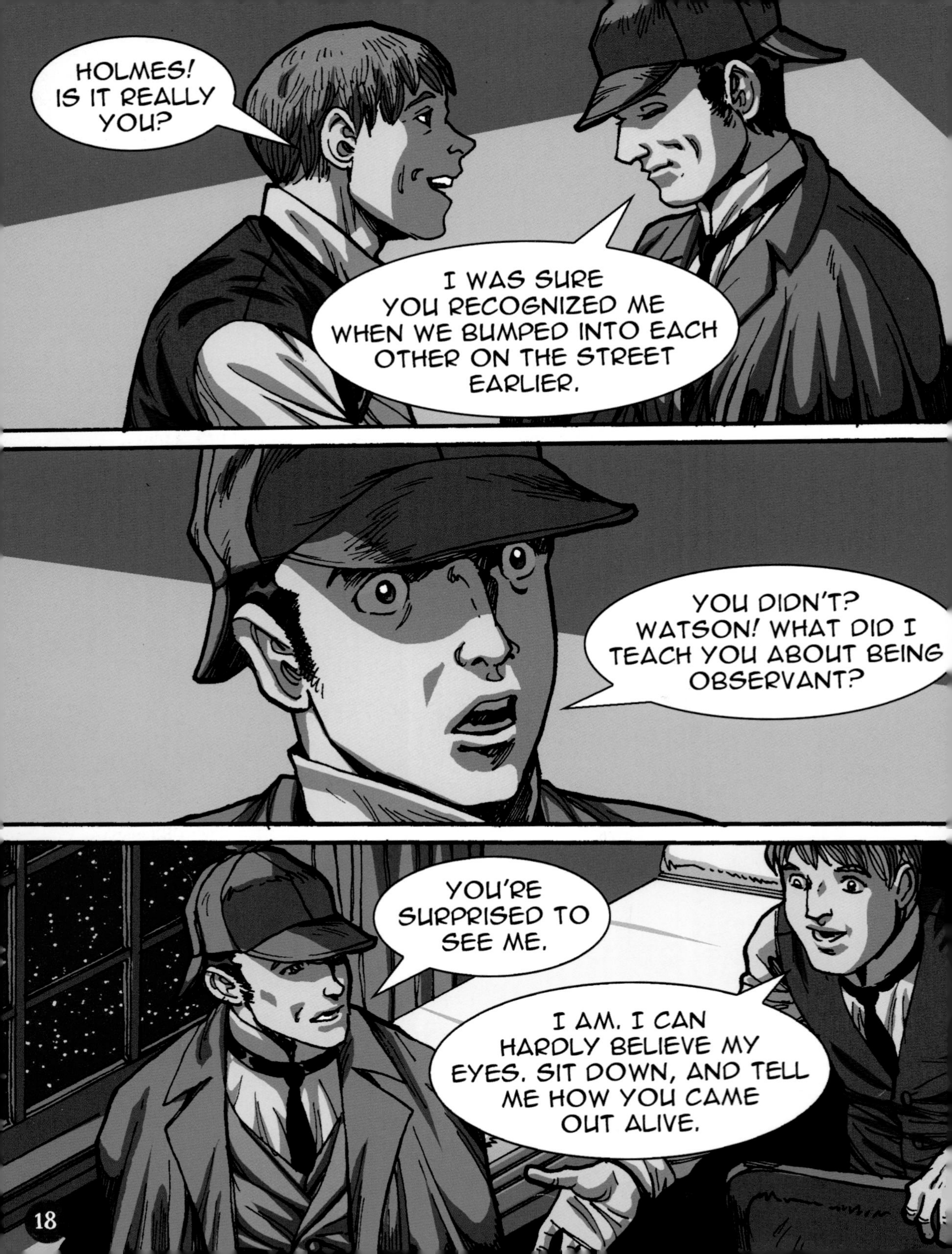
HOLMES! IS IT REALLY YOU?
I WAS SURE YOU RECOGNIZED ME WHEN WE BUMPED INTO EACH OTHER ON THE STREET EARLIER.
YOU DIDN'T? WATSON! WHAT DID I TEACH YOU ABOUT BEING OBSERVANT?
YOU'RE SURPRISED TO SEE ME.
I AM. I CAN HARDLY BELIEVE MY EYES. SIT DOWN, AND TELL ME HOW YOU CAME OUT ALIVE.

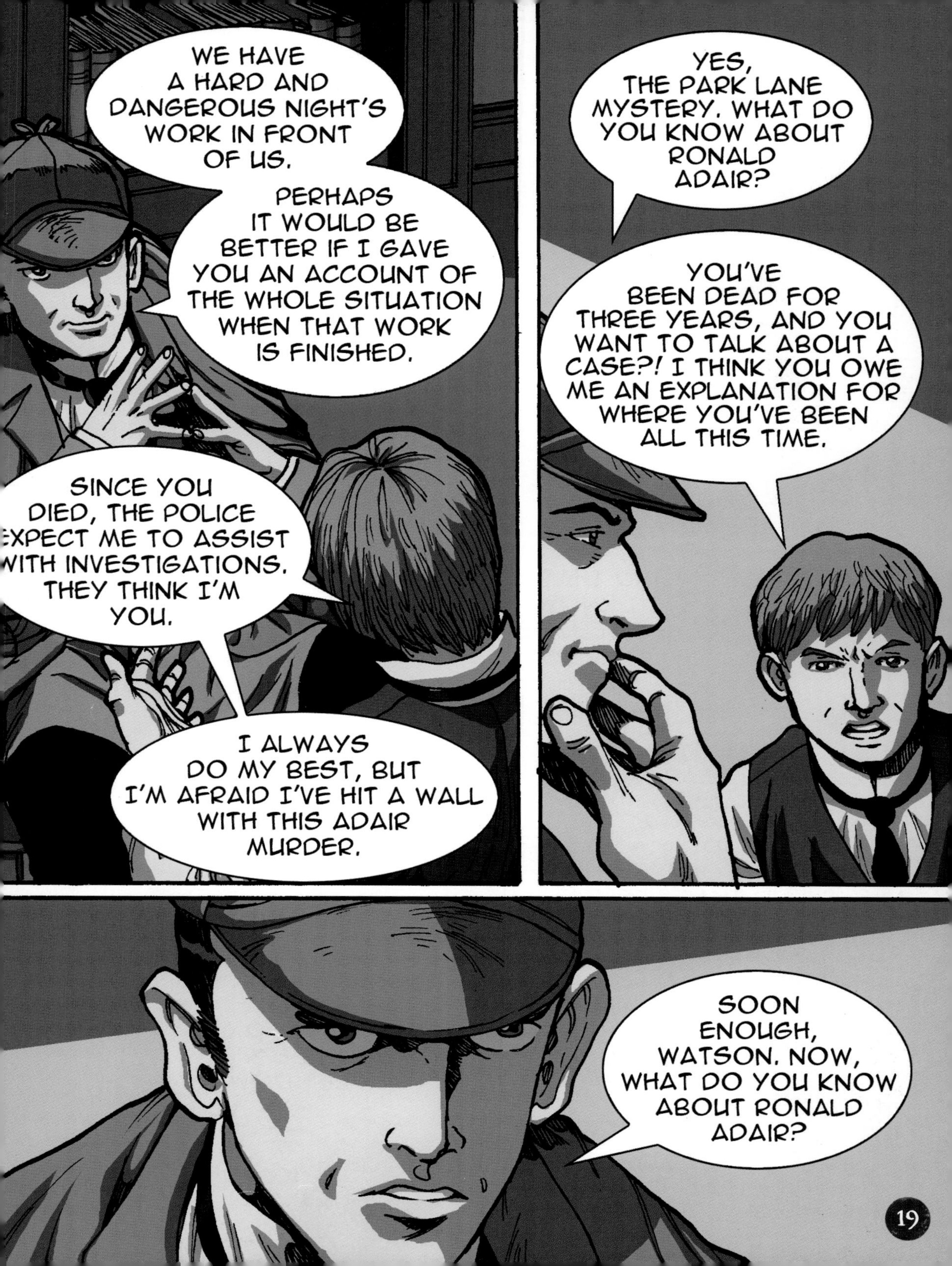
WE HAVE A HARD AND DANGEROUS NIGHT'S WORK IN FRONT OF US.
PERHAPS IT WOULD BE BETTER IF I GAVE YOU AN ACCOUNT OF THE WHOLE SITUATION WHEN THAT WORK IS FINISHED.
SINCE YOU DIED, THE POLICE EXPECT ME TO ASSIST WITH INVESTIGATIONS. THEY THINK I'M YOU.
I ALWAYS DO MY BEST, BUT I'M AFRAID I'VE HIT A WALL WITH THIS ADAIR MURDER.
YES, THE PARK LANE MYSTERY. WHAT DO YOU KNOW ABOUT RONALD ADAIR?
YOU'VE BEEN DEAD FOR THREE YEARS, AND YOU WANT TO TALK ABOUT A CASE?! I THINK YOU OWE ME AN EXPLANATION FOR WHERE YOU'VE BEEN ALL THIS TIME.
SOON ENOUGH, WATSON. NOW, WHAT DO YOU KNOW ABOUT RONALD ADAIR?

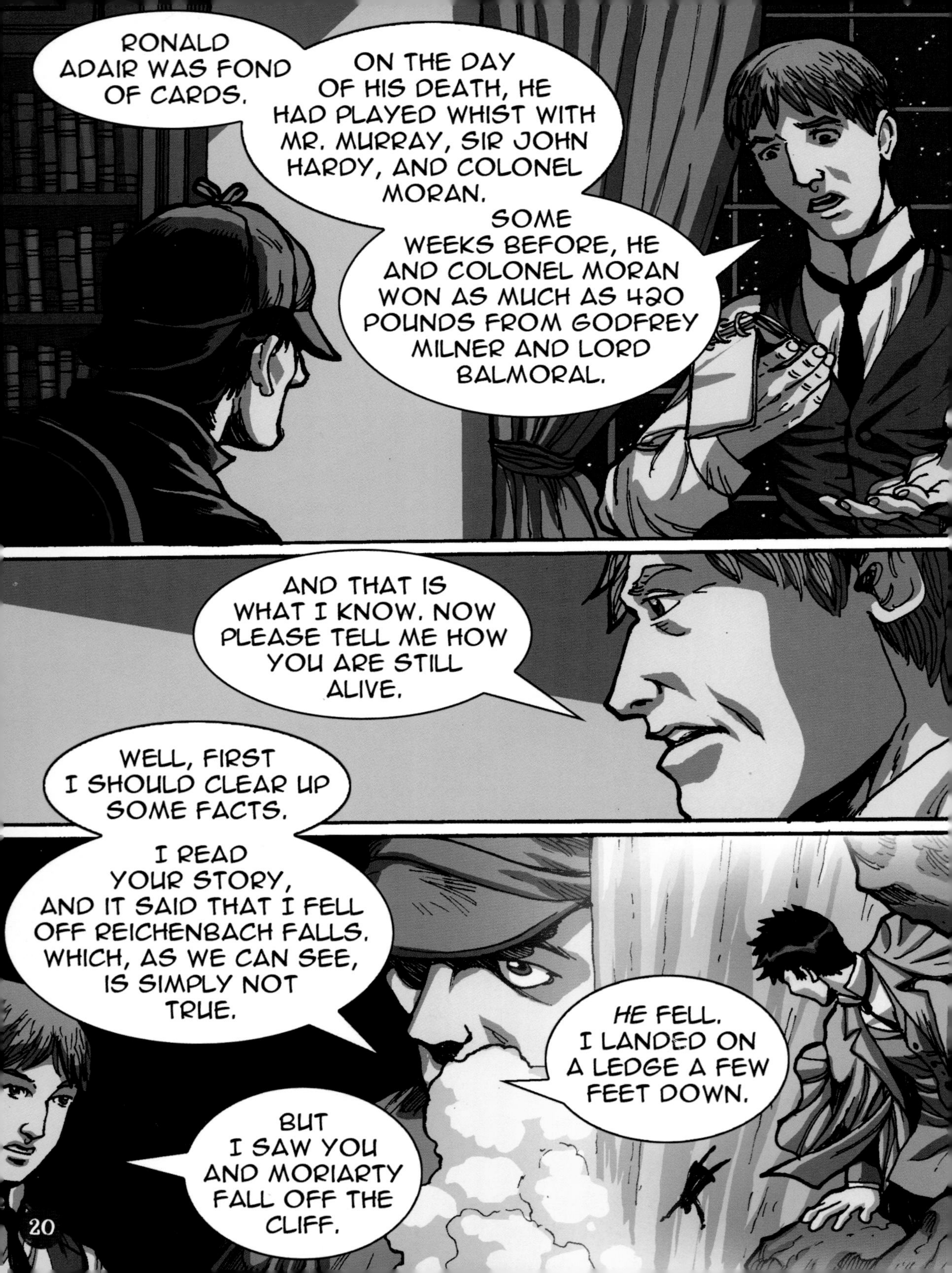
RONALD ADAIR WAS FOND OF CARDS.
ON THE DAY OF HIS DEATH, HE HAD PLAYED WHIST WITH MR. MURRAY, SIR JOHN HARDY, AND COLONEL MORAN.
SOME WEEKS BEFORE, HE AND COLONEL MORAN WON AS MUCH AS 420 POUNDS FROM GODFREY MILNER AND LORD BALMORAL.
AND THAT IS WHAT I KNOW. NOW PLEASE TELL ME HOW YOU ARE STILL ALIVE.
WELL, FIRST I SHOULD CLEAR UP SOME FACTS.
I READ YOUR STORY, AND IT SAID THAT I FELL OFF REICHENBACH FALLS. WHICH, AS WE CAN SEE, IS SIMPLY NOT TRUE.
BUT I SAW YOU AND MORIARTY FALL OFF THE CLIFF.
HE FELL. I LANDED ON A LEDGE A FEW FEET DOWN.

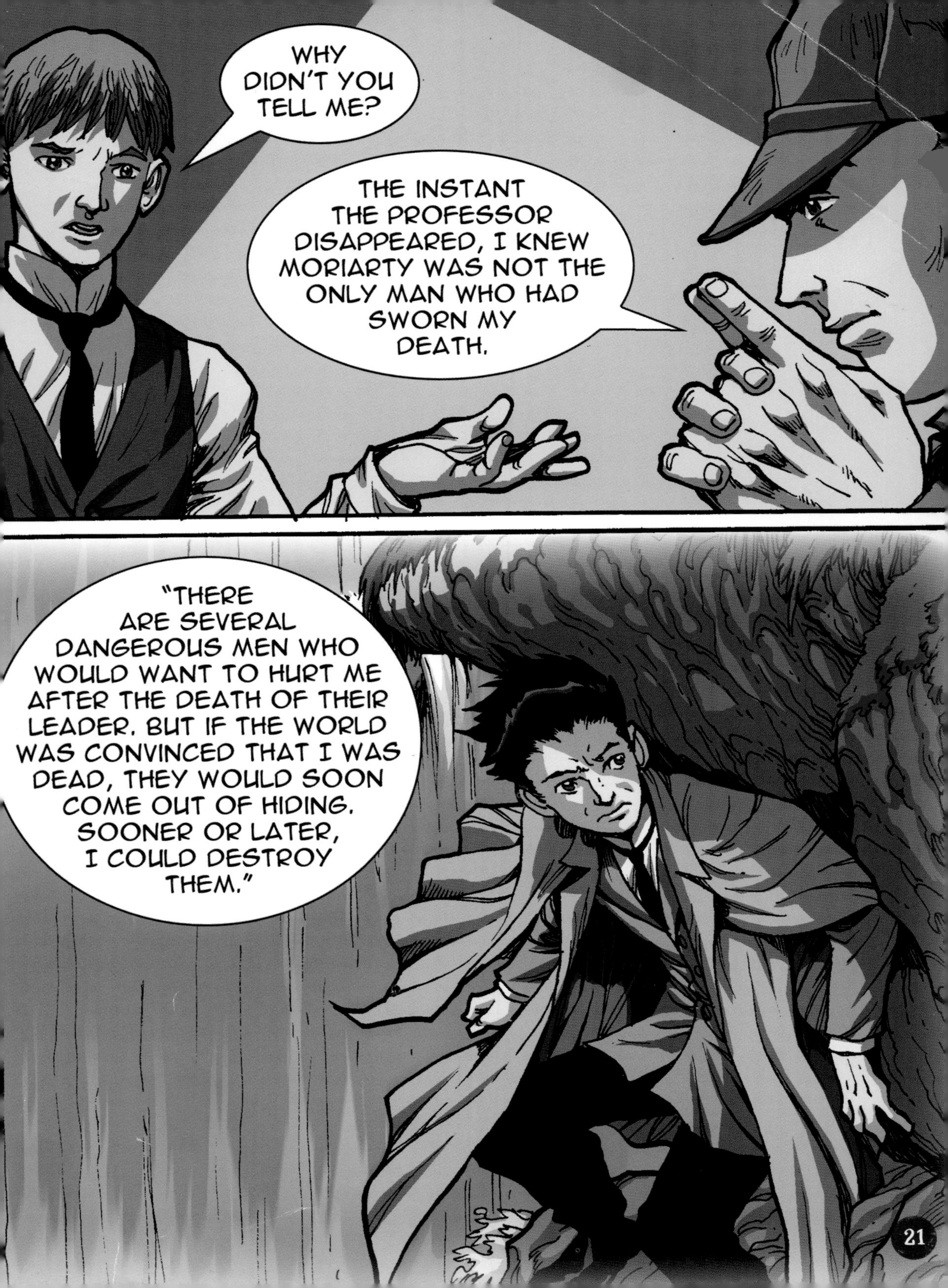
WHY DIDN'T YOU TELL ME?
THE INSTANT THE PROFESSOR DISAPPEARED, I KNEW MORIARTY WAS NOT THE ONLY MAN WHO HAD SWORN MY DEATH.
"THERE ARE SEVERAL DANGEROUS MEN WHO WOULD WANT TO HURT ME AFTER THE DEATH OF THEIR LEADER. BUT IF THE WORLD WAS CONVINCED THAT I WAS DEAD, THEY WOULD SOON COME OUT OF HIDING. SOONER OR LATER, I COULD DESTROY THEM."

"I MUST SAY, YOUR INVESTIGATION OF MY DEATH WAS INADEQUATE."

"YOU LOOKED AROUND FOR TWO MINUTES, FORMED A WRONG CONCLUSION AND DEPARTED FOR THE HOTEL."

"I IMAGINED THAT I HAD REACHED THE END OF MY ADVENTURES."

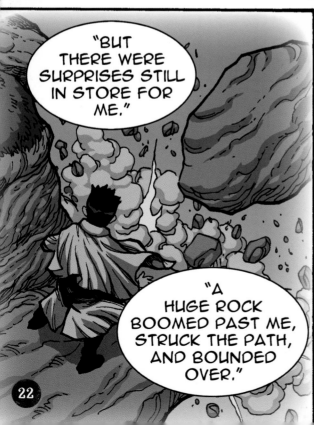

"BUT THERE WERE SURPRISES STILL IN STORE FOR ME."

"A HUGE ROCK BOOMED PAST ME, STRUCK THE PATH, AND BOUNDED OVER."

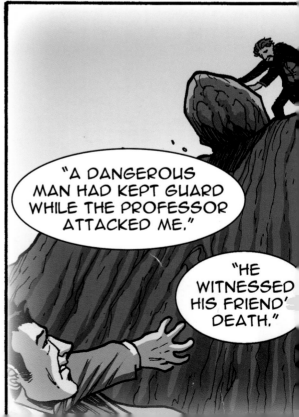

"A DANGEROUS MAN HAD KEPT GUARD WHILE THE PROFESSOR ATTACKED ME."

"HE WITNESSED HIS FRIEND' DEATH."

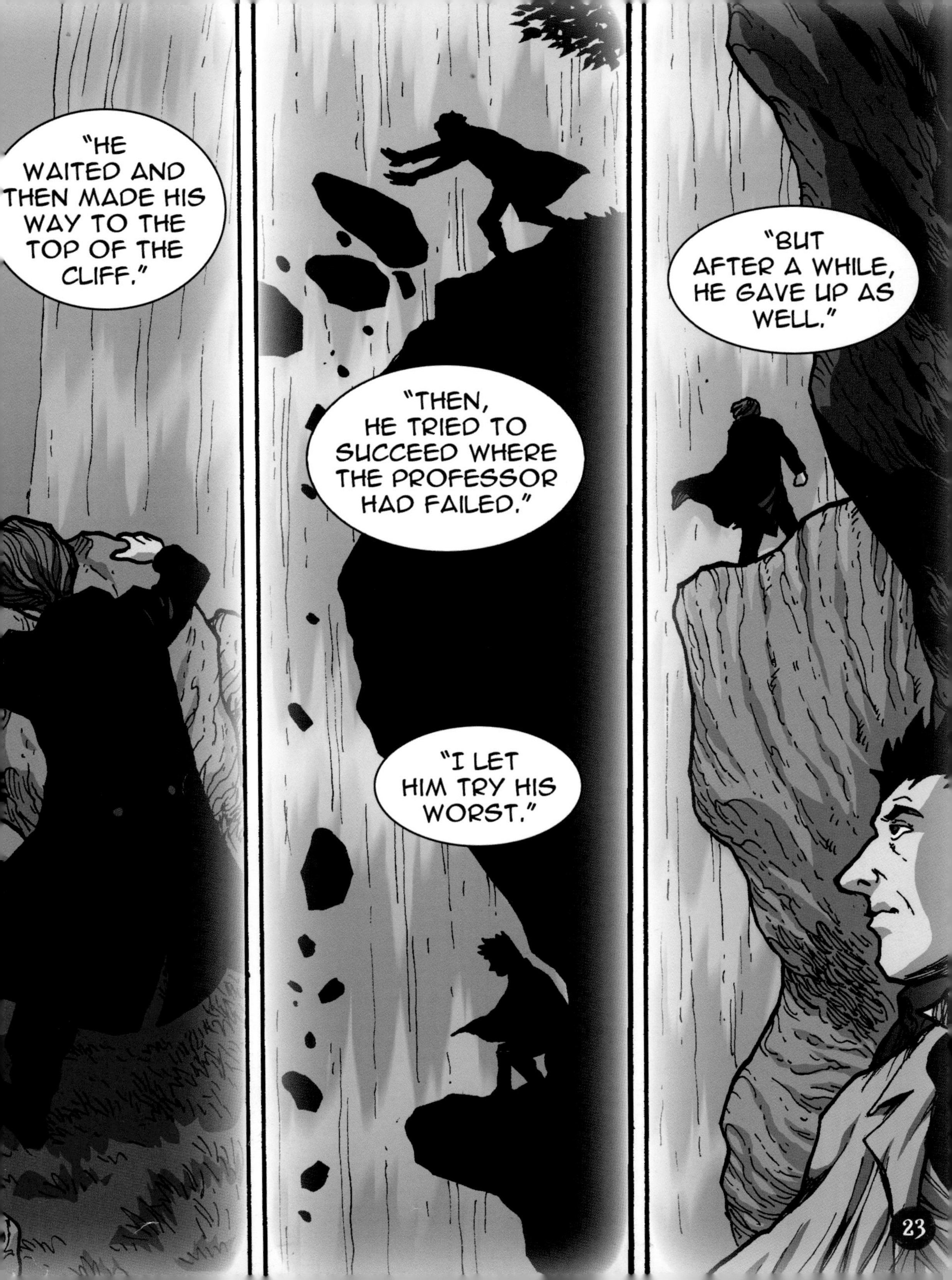
"HE WAITED AND THEN MADE HIS WAY TO THE TOP OF THE CLIFF."
"THEN, HE TRIED TO SUCCEED WHERE THE PROFESSOR HAD FAILED."
"I LET HIM TRY HIS WORST."
"BUT AFTER A WHILE, HE GAVE UP AS WELL."

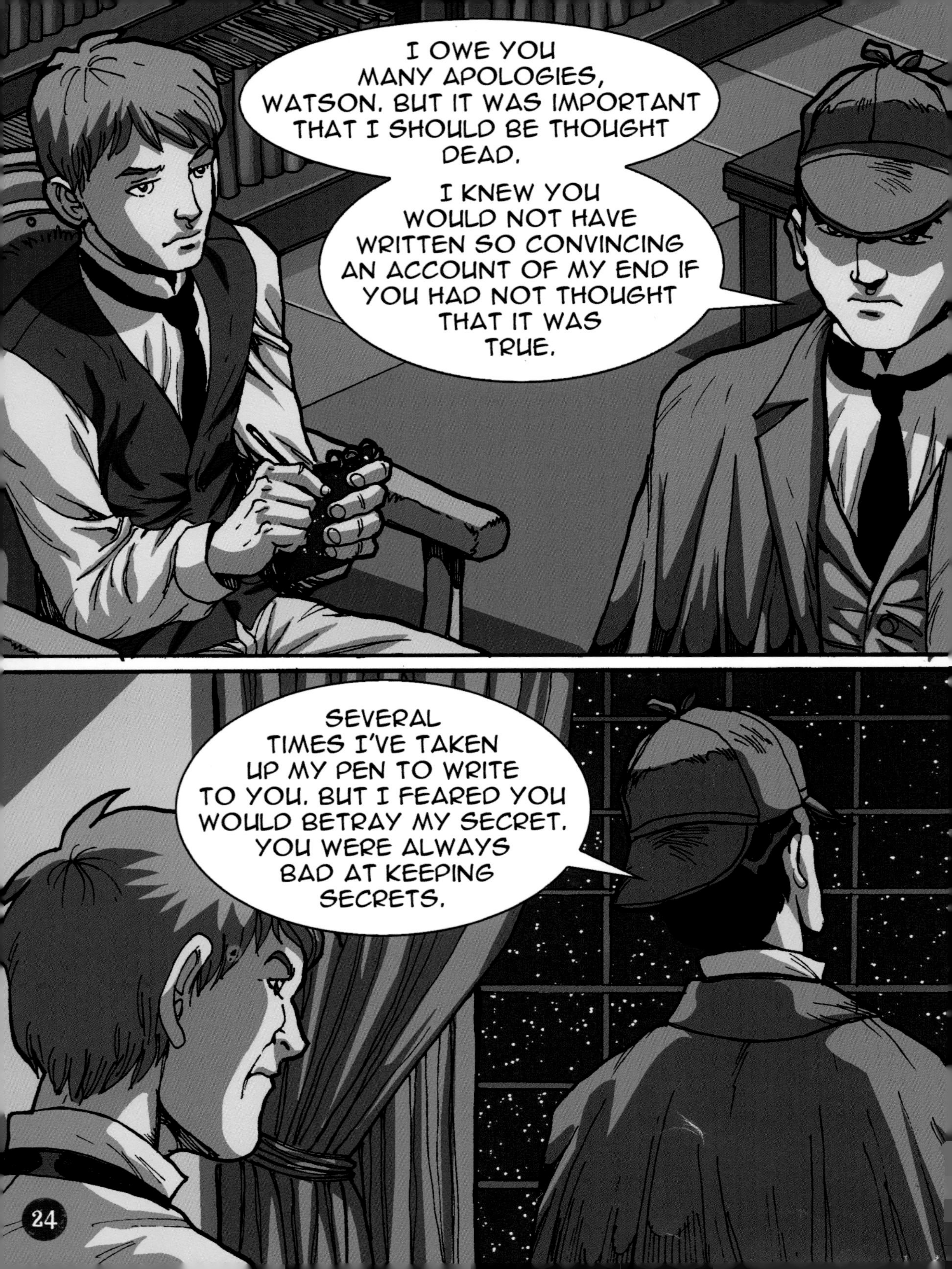
I OWE YOU MANY APOLOGIES, WATSON. BUT IT WAS IMPORTANT THAT I SHOULD BE THOUGHT DEAD.
I KNEW YOU WOULD NOT HAVE WRITTEN SO CONVINCING AN ACCOUNT OF MY END IF YOU HAD NOT THOUGHT THAT IT WAS TRUE.
SEVERAL TIMES I'VE TAKEN UP MY PEN TO WRITE TO YOU. BUT I FEARED YOU WOULD BETRAY MY SECRET. YOU WERE ALWAYS BAD AT KEEPING SECRETS.

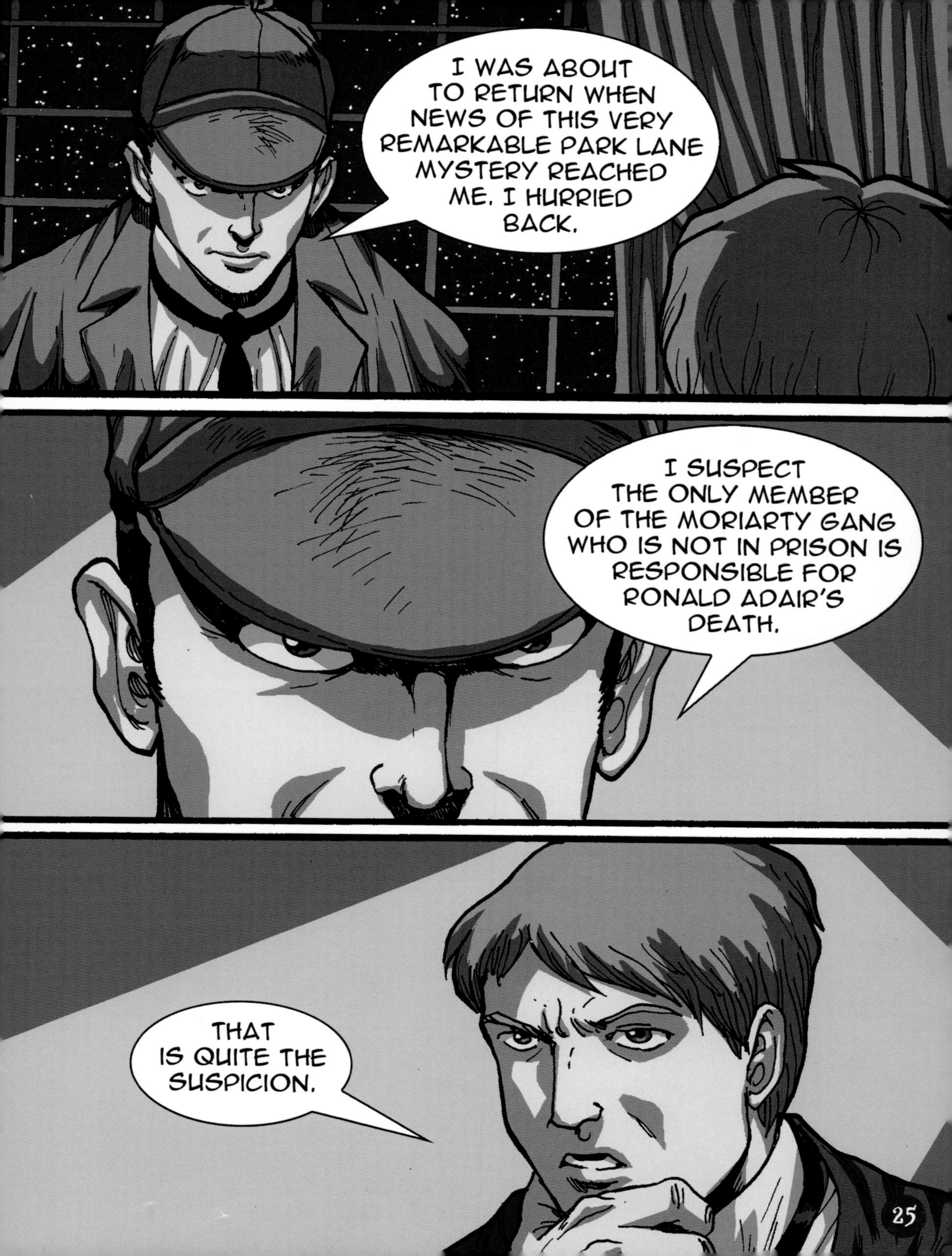
I WAS ABOUT TO RETURN WHEN NEWS OF THIS VERY REMARKABLE PARK LANE MYSTERY REACHED ME. I HURRIED BACK.
I SUSPECT THE ONLY MEMBER OF THE MORIARTY GANG WHO IS NOT IN PRISON IS RESPONSIBLE FOR RONALD ADAIR'S DEATH.
THAT IS QUITE THE SUSPICION.

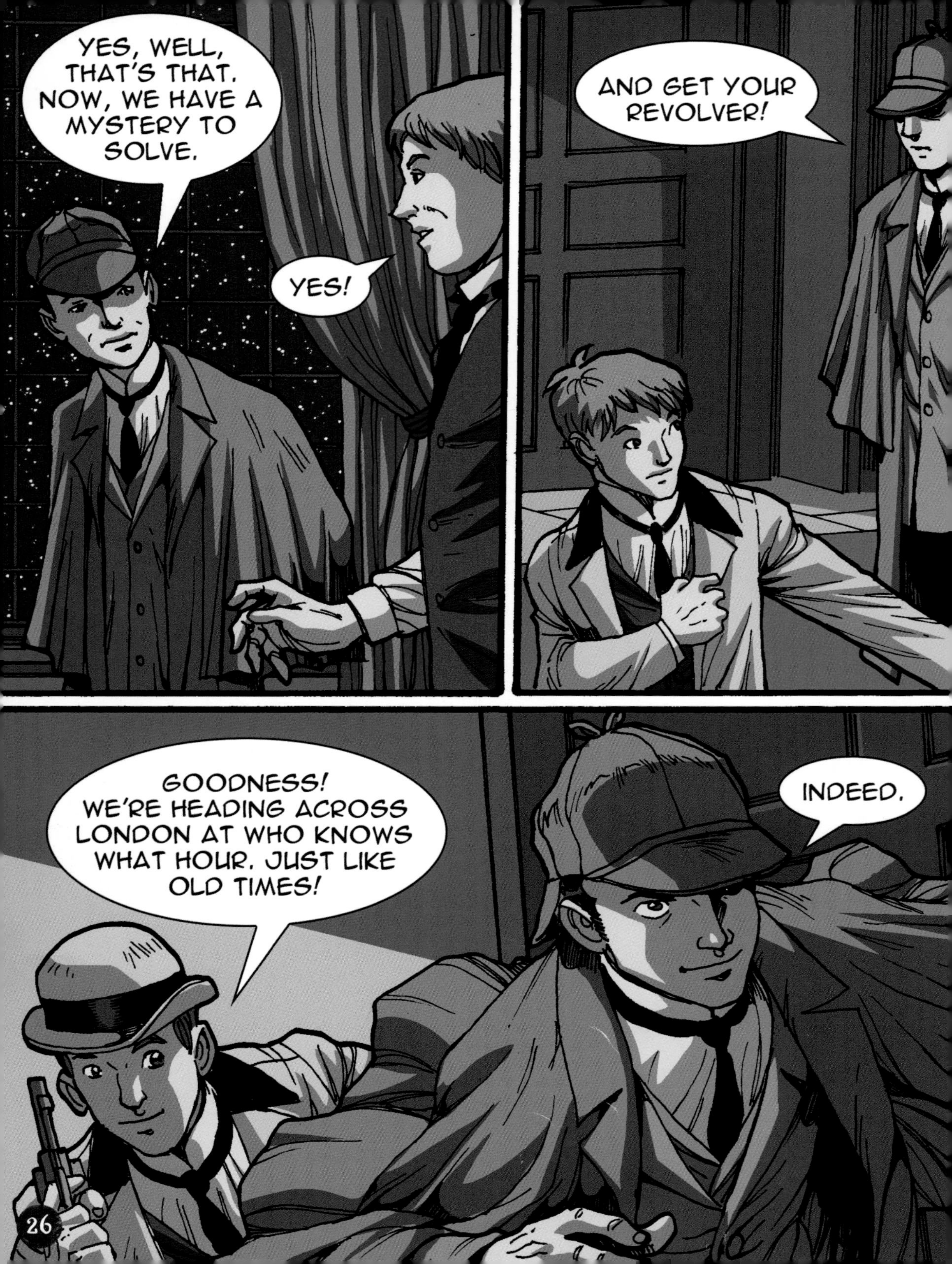
YES, WELL, THAT'S THAT. NOW, WE HAVE A MYSTERY TO SOLVE.
YES!
AND GET YOUR REVOLVER!
GOODNESS! WE'RE HEADING ACROSS LONDON AT WHO KNOWS WHAT HOUR. JUST LIKE OLD TIMES!
INDEED.

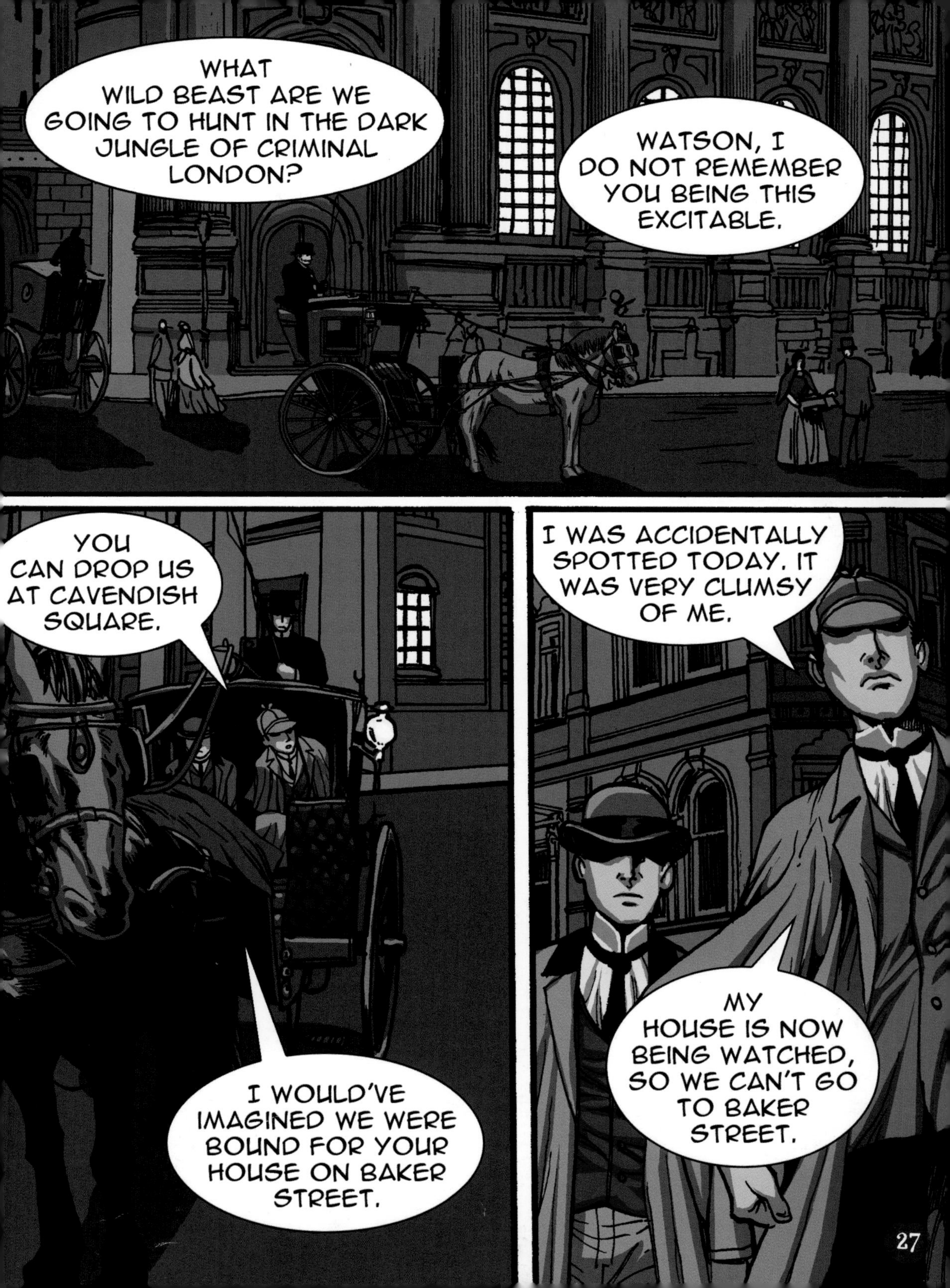
WHAT WILD BEAST ARE WE GOING TO HUNT IN THE DARK JUNGLE OF CRIMINAL LONDON?
WATSON, I DO NOT REMEMBER YOU BEING THIS EXCITABLE.
YOU CAN DROP US AT CAVENDISH SQUARE.
I WOULD'VE IMAGINED WE WERE BOUND FOR YOUR HOUSE ON BAKER STREET.
I WAS ACCIDENTALLY SPOTTED TODAY. IT WAS VERY CLUMSY OF ME.
MY HOUSE IS NOW BEING WATCHED, SO WE CAN'T GO TO BAKER STREET.

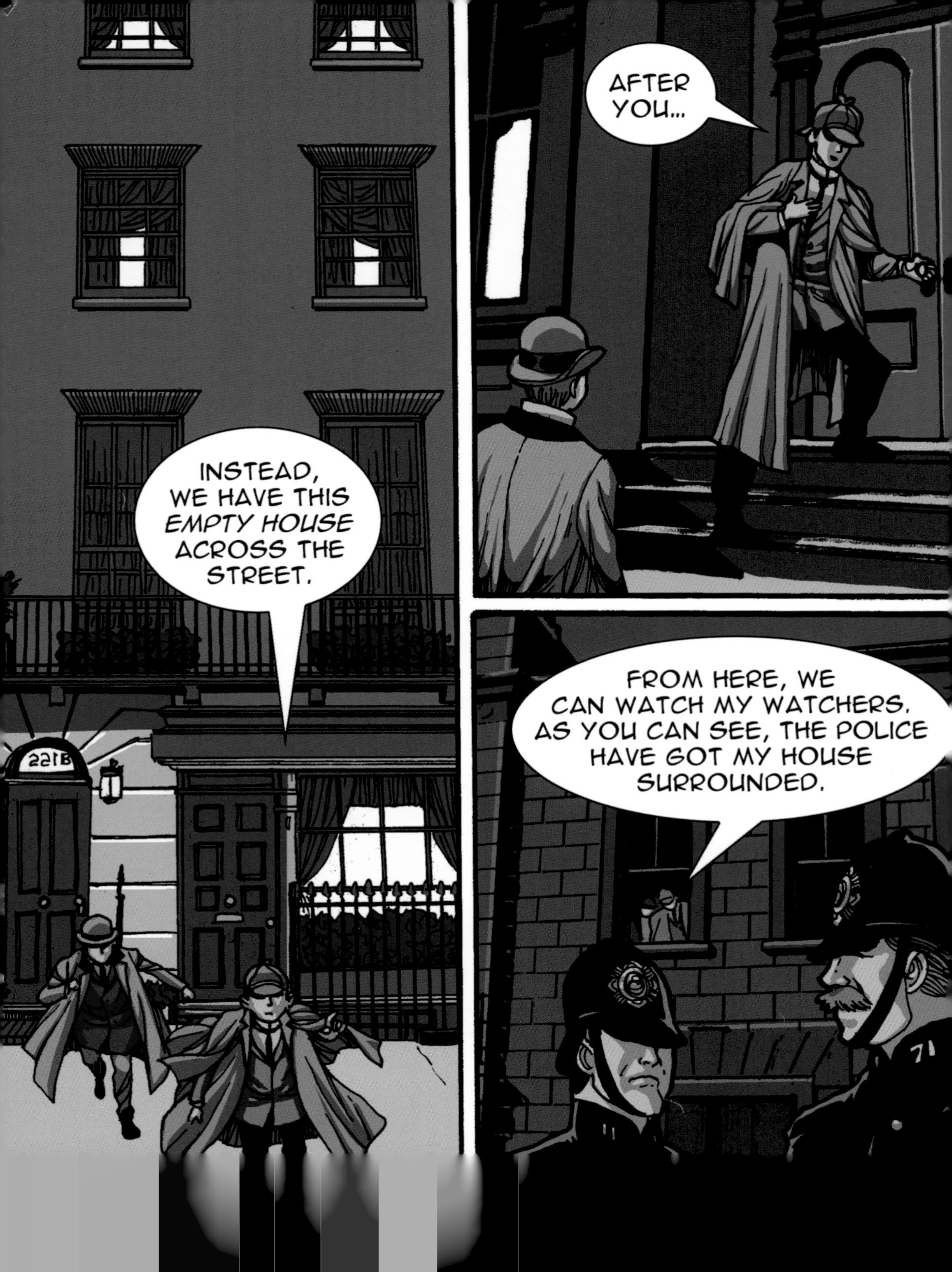

INSTEAD, WE HAVE THIS *EMPTY HOUSE* ACROSS THE STREET.
221B
AFTER YOU...
FROM HERE, WE CAN WATCH MY WATCHERS. AS YOU CAN SEE, THE POLICE HAVE GOT MY HOUSE SURROUNDED.
71

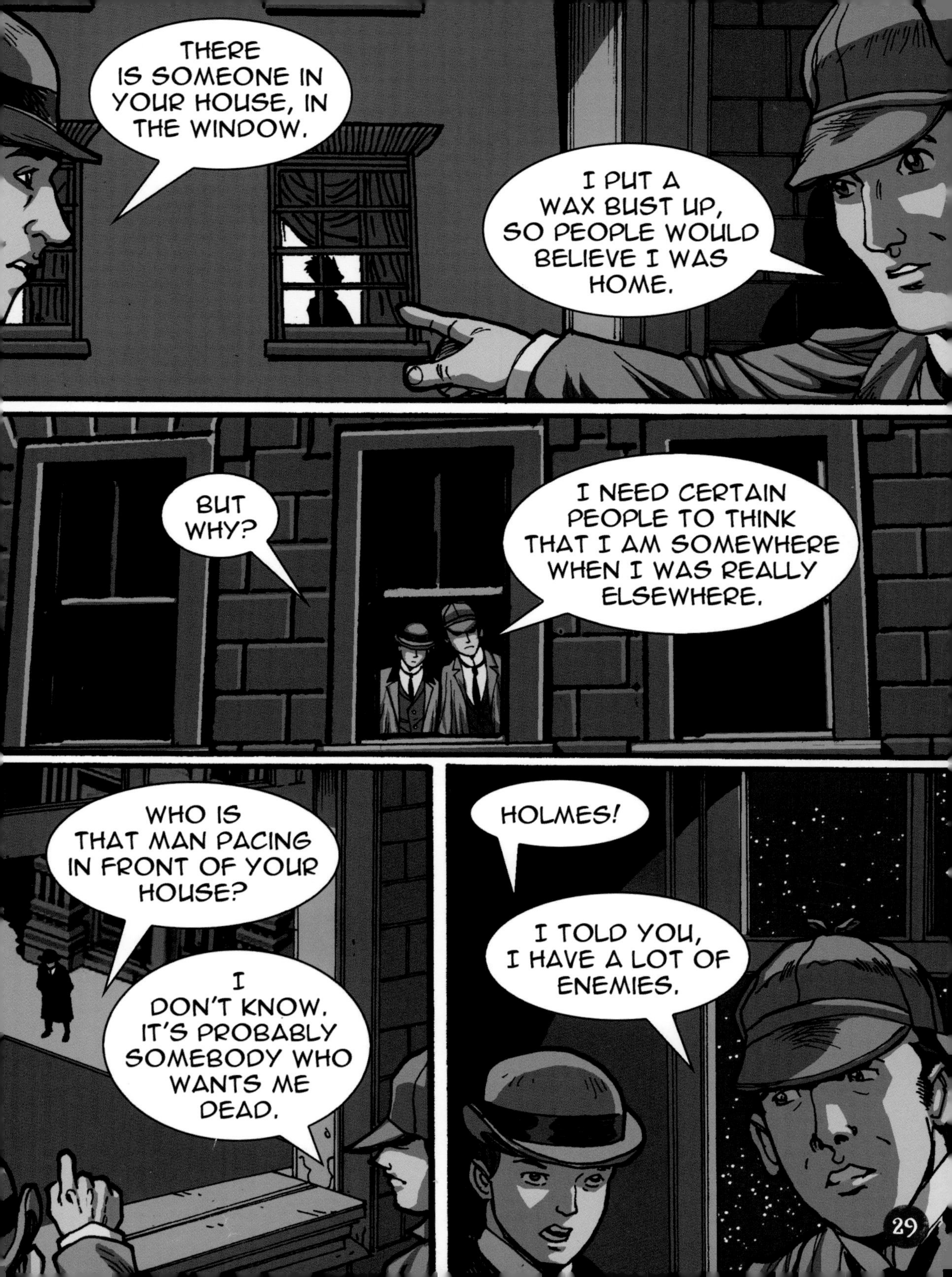
THERE IS SOMEONE IN YOUR HOUSE, IN THE WINDOW.
I PUT A WAX BUST UP, SO PEOPLE WOULD BELIEVE I WAS HOME.
BUT WHY?
I NEED CERTAIN PEOPLE TO THINK THAT I AM SOMEWHERE WHEN I WAS REALLY ELSEWHERE.
WHO IS THAT MAN PACING IN FRONT OF YOUR HOUSE?
I DON'T KNOW. IT'S PROBABLY SOMEBODY WHO WANTS ME DEAD.
HOLMES!
I TOLD YOU, I HAVE A LOT OF ENEMIES.

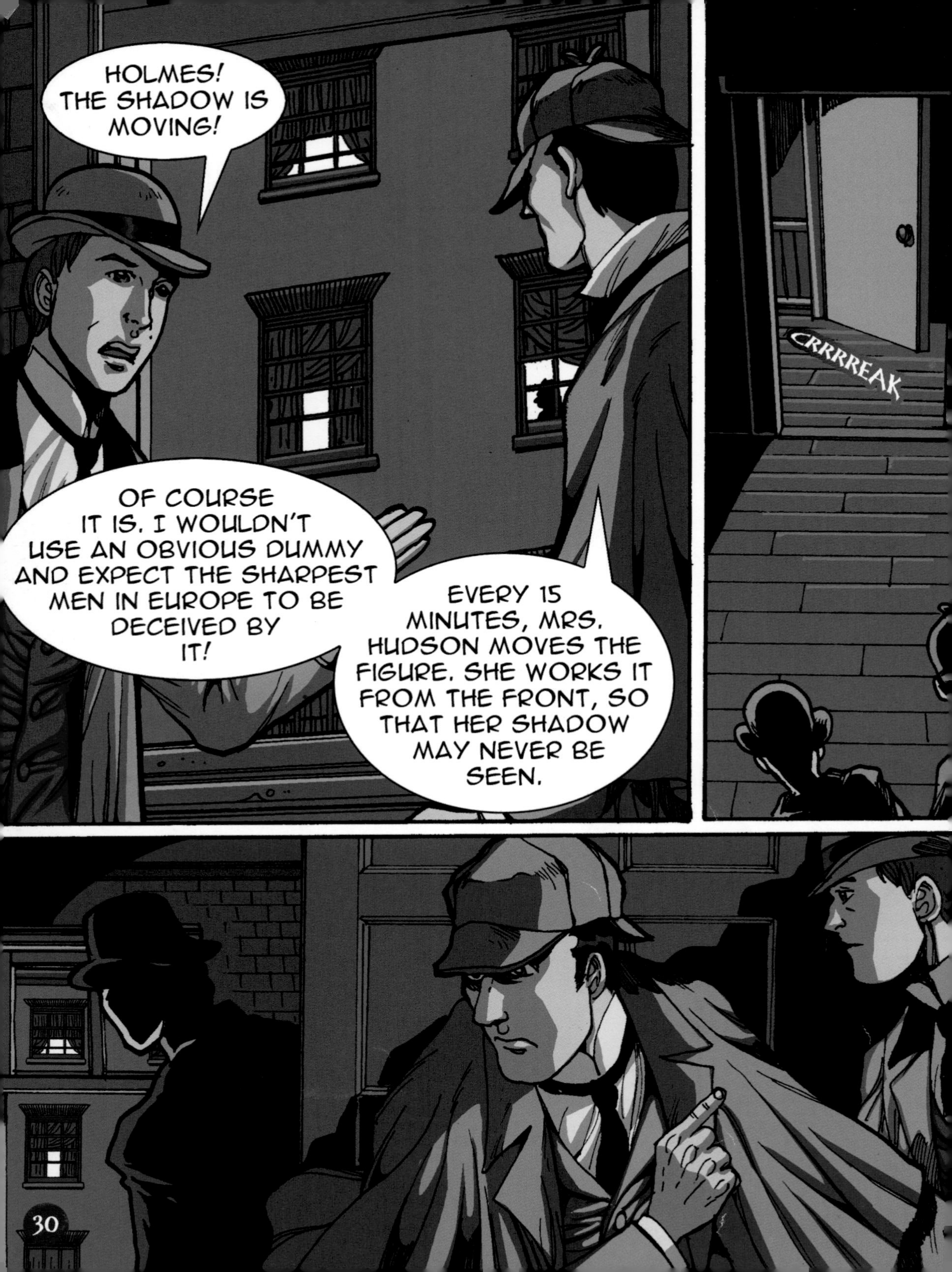
HOLMES! THE SHADOW IS MOVING!
OF COURSE IT IS. I WOULDN'T USE AN OBVIOUS DUMMY AND EXPECT THE SHARPEST MEN IN EUROPE TO BE DECEIVED BY IT!
EVERY 15 MINUTES, MRS. HUDSON MOVES THE FIGURE. SHE WORKS IT FROM THE FRONT, SO THAT HER SHADOW MAY NEVER BE SEEN.
CRRRREAK

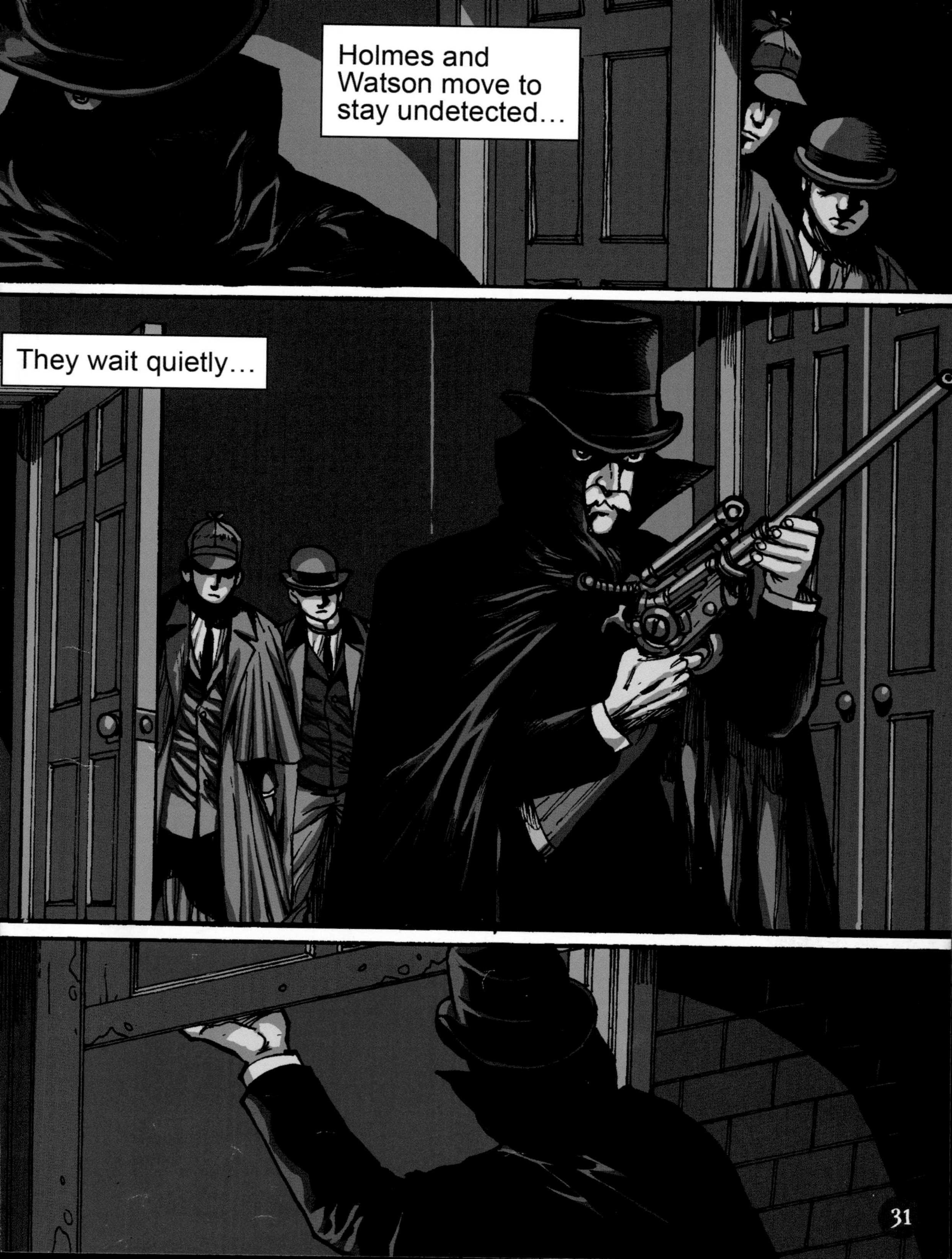
Holmes and Watson move to stay undetected…
They wait quietly…

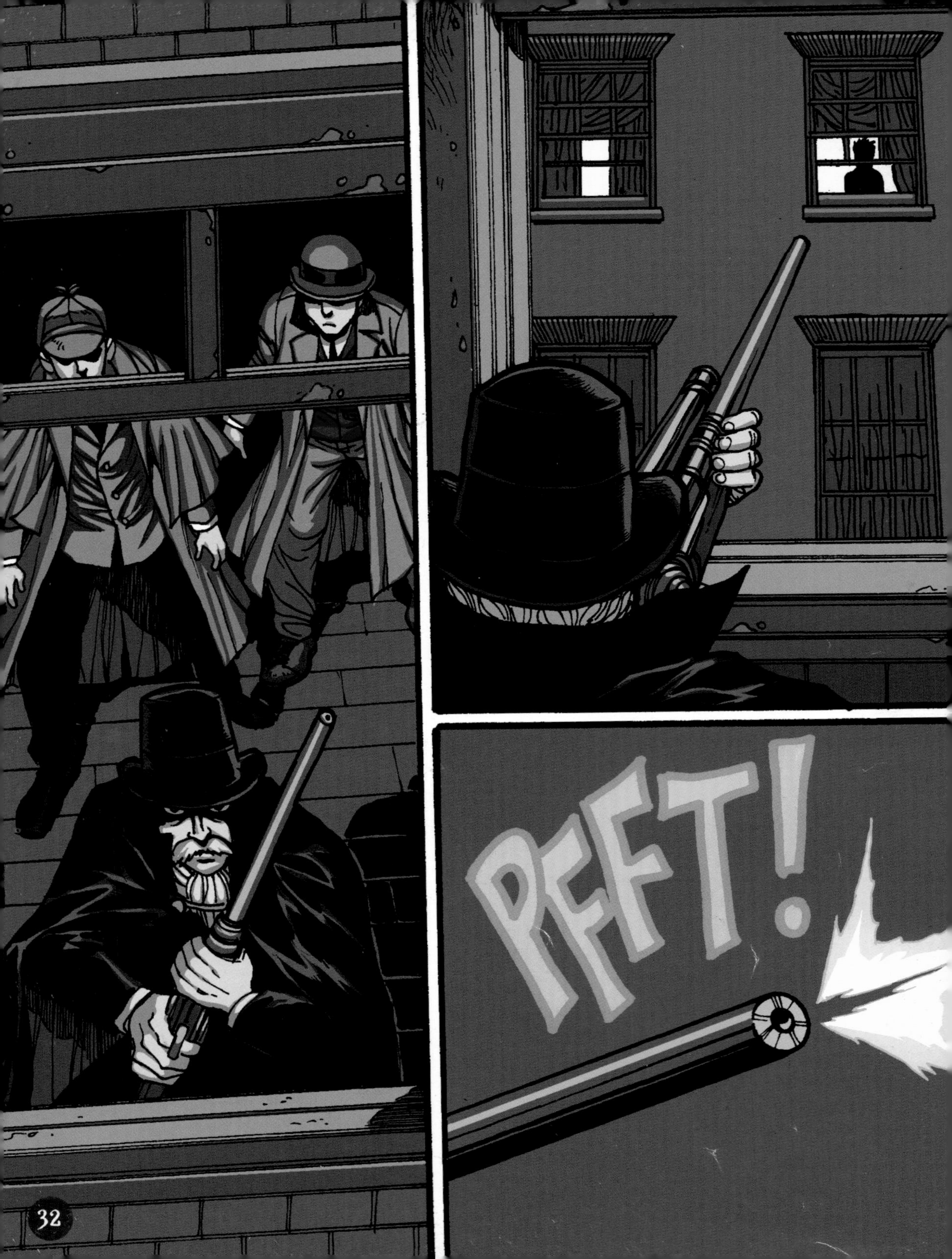
PFFT!

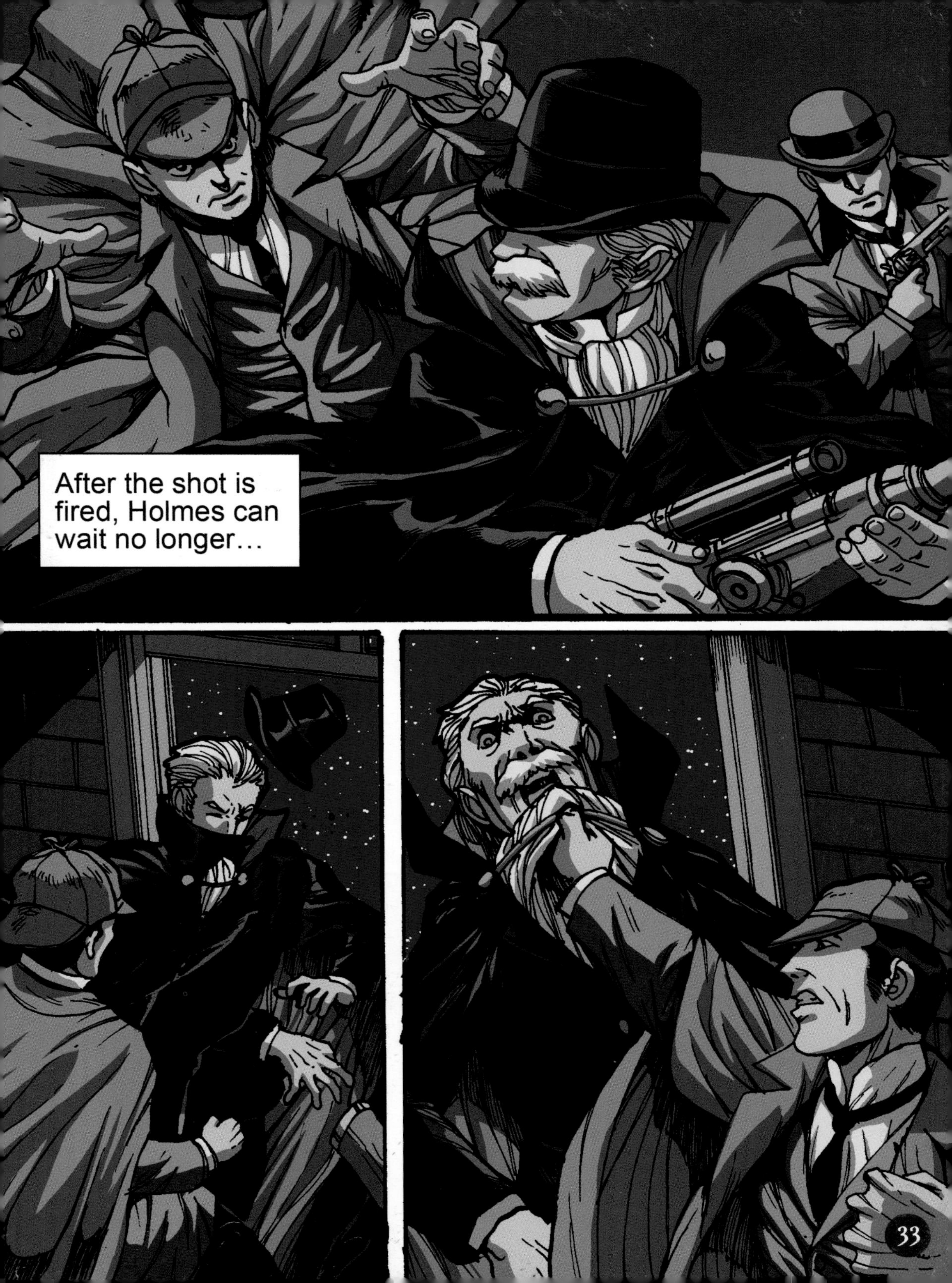
After the shot is fired, Holmes can wait no longer…

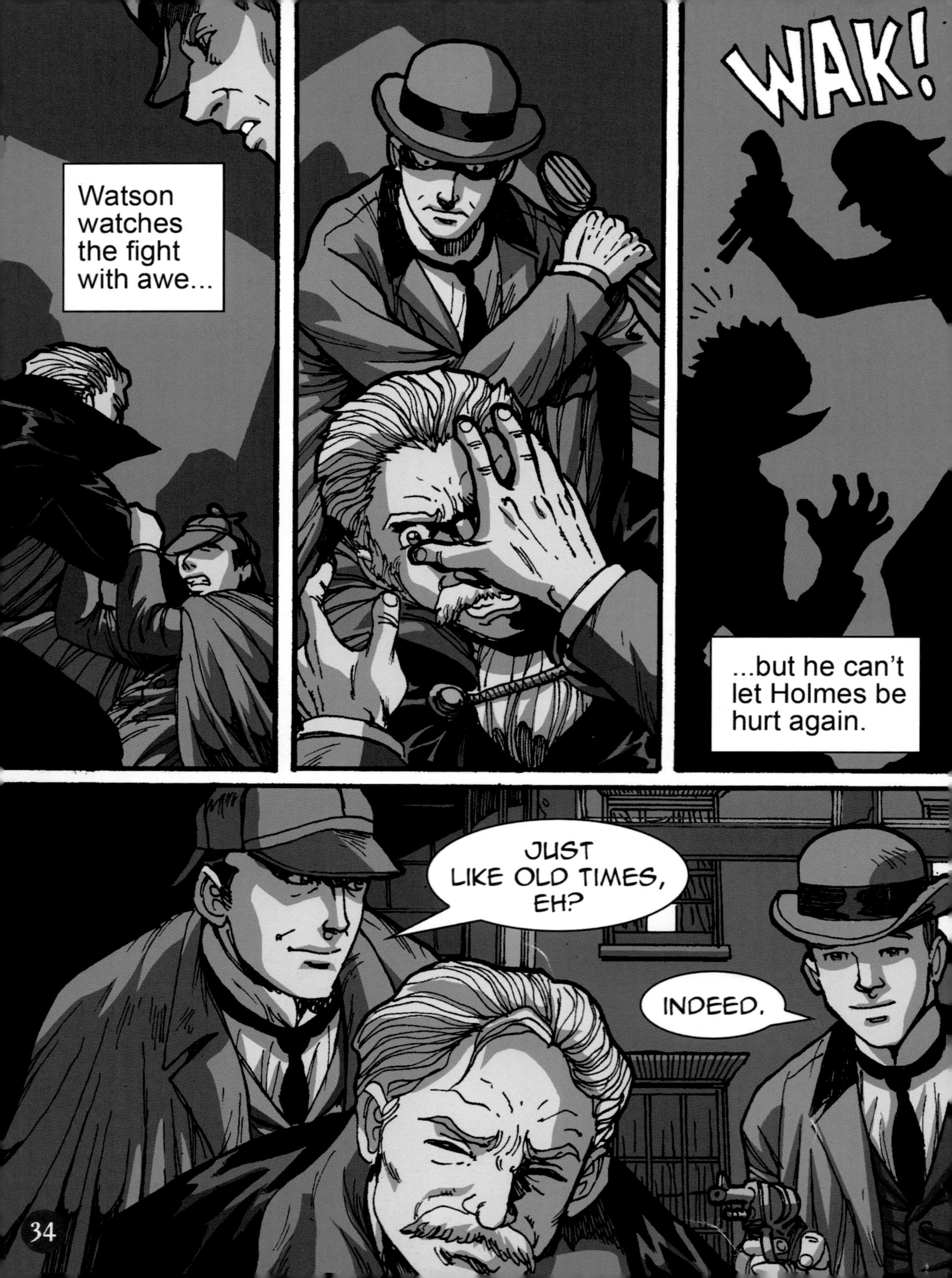
Watson watches the fight with awe...
WAK!
...but he can't let Holmes be hurt again.
JUST LIKE OLD TIMES, EH?
INDEED.

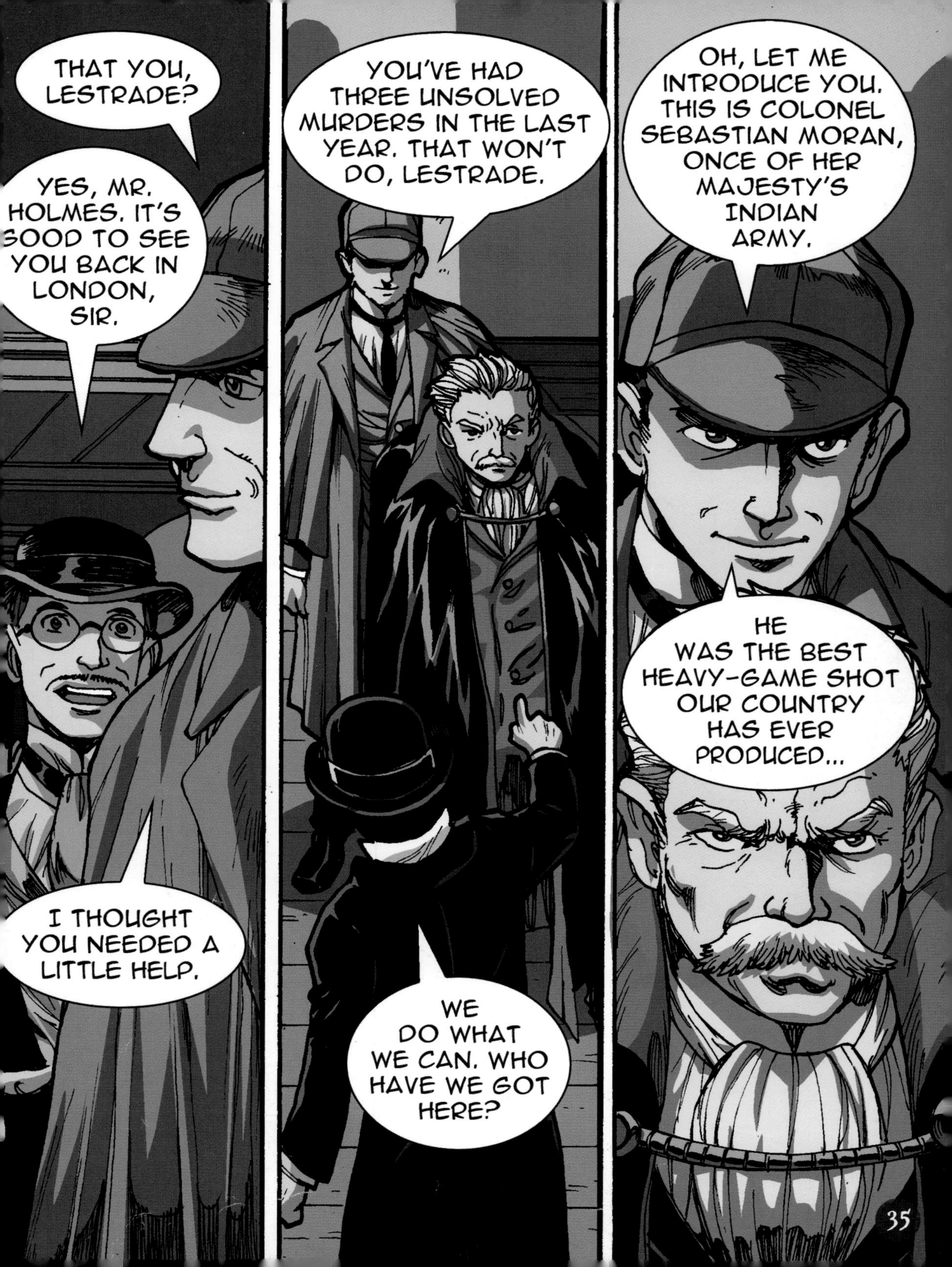
THAT YOU, LESTRADE?
YES, MR. HOLMES. IT'S GOOD TO SEE YOU BACK IN LONDON, SIR.
I THOUGHT YOU NEEDED A LITTLE HELP.
YOU'VE HAD THREE UNSOLVED MURDERS IN THE LAST YEAR. THAT WON'T DO, LESTRADE.
WE DO WHAT WE CAN. WHO HAVE WE GOT HERE?
OH, LET ME INTRODUCE YOU. THIS IS COLONEL SEBASTIAN MORAN, ONCE OF HER MAJESTY'S INDIAN ARMY.
HE WAS THE BEST HEAVY-GAME SHOT OUR COUNTRY HAS EVER PRODUCED...

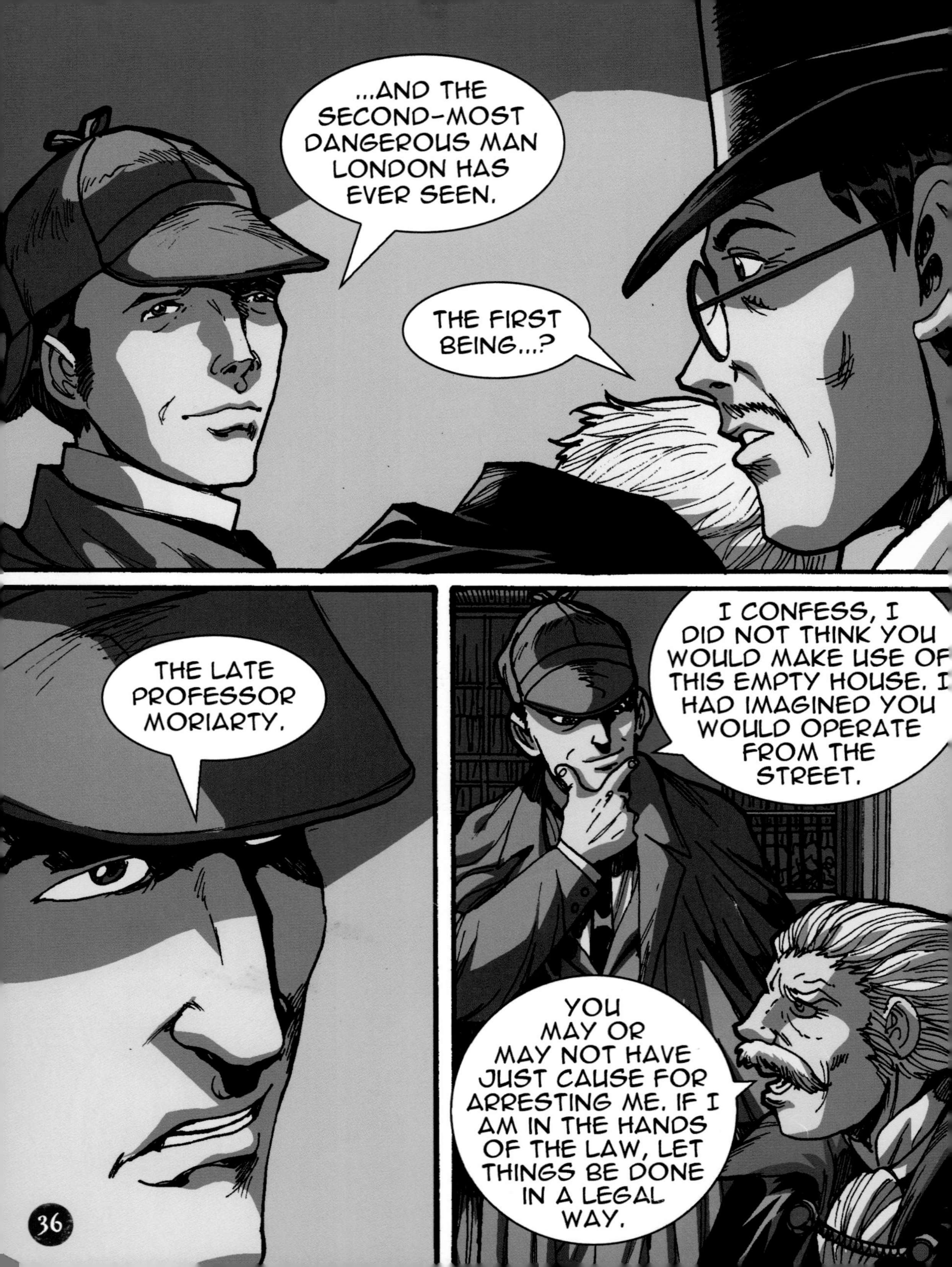
...AND THE SECOND-MOST DANGEROUS MAN LONDON HAS EVER SEEN.
THE FIRST BEING...?
THE LATE PROFESSOR MORIARTY.
I CONFESS, I DID NOT THINK YOU WOULD MAKE USE OF THIS EMPTY HOUSE. I HAD IMAGINED YOU WOULD OPERATE FROM THE STREET.
YOU MAY OR MAY NOT HAVE JUST CAUSE FOR ARRESTING ME. IF I AM IN THE HANDS OF THE LAW, LET THINGS BE DONE IN A LEGAL WAY.

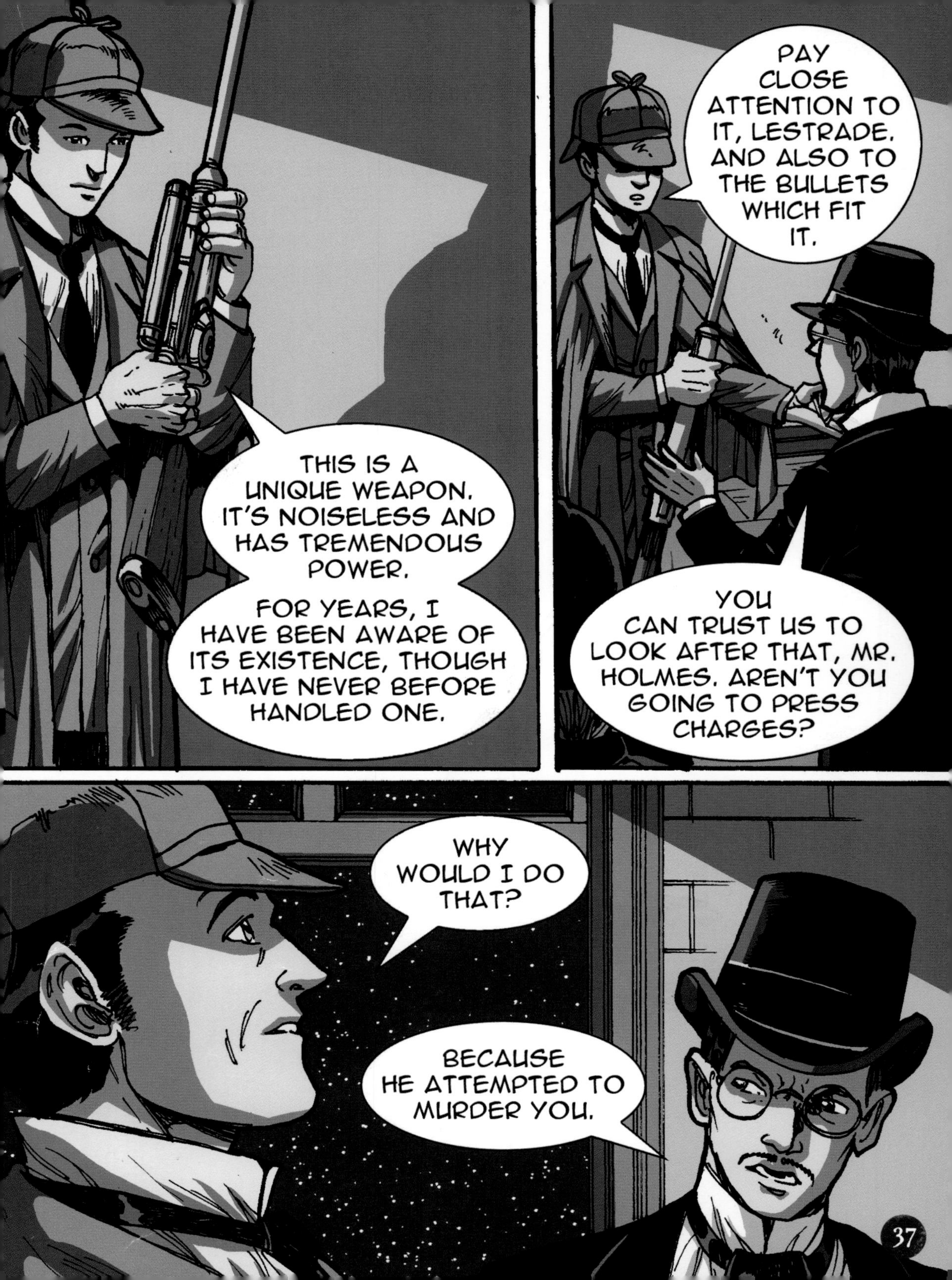
THIS IS A UNIQUE WEAPON. IT'S NOISELESS AND HAS TREMENDOUS POWER.
FOR YEARS, I HAVE BEEN AWARE OF ITS EXISTENCE, THOUGH I HAVE NEVER BEFORE HANDLED ONE.
PAY CLOSE ATTENTION TO IT, LESTRADE. AND ALSO TO THE BULLETS WHICH FIT IT.
YOU CAN TRUST US TO LOOK AFTER THAT, MR. HOLMES. AREN'T YOU GOING TO PRESS CHARGES?
WHY WOULD I DO THAT?
BECAUSE HE ATTEMPTED TO MURDER YOU.

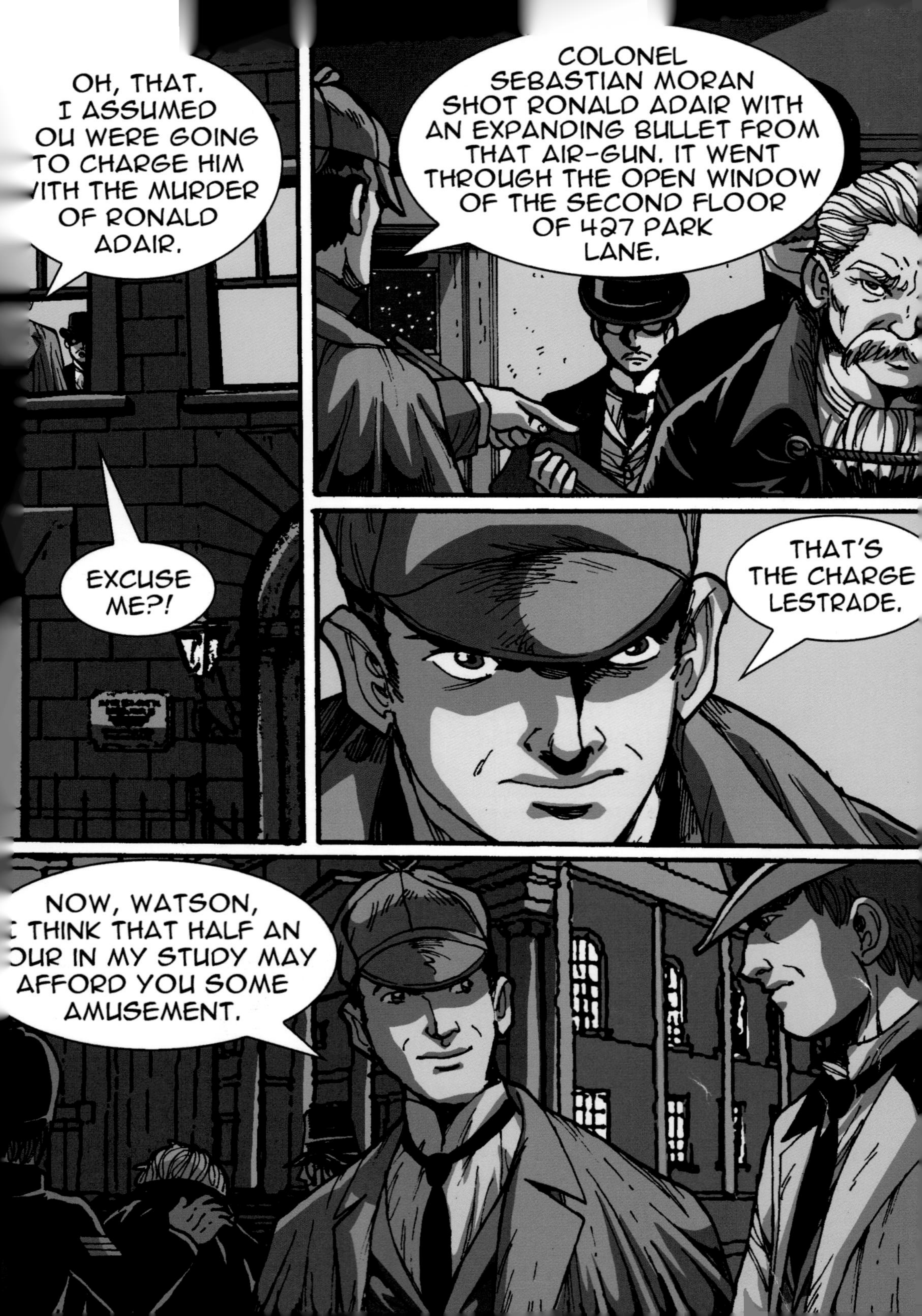
OH, THAT. I ASSUMED OU WERE GOING TO CHARGE HIM WITH THE MURDER OF RONALD ADAIR.
COLONEL SEBASTIAN MORAN SHOT RONALD ADAIR WITH AN EXPANDING BULLET FROM THAT AIR-GUN. IT WENT THROUGH THE OPEN WINDOW OF THE SECOND FLOOR OF 427 PARK LANE.
EXCUSE ME?!
THAT'S THE CHARGE LESTRADE.
NOW, WATSON, I THINK THAT HALF AN OUR IN MY STUDY MAY AFFORD YOU SOME AMUSEMENT.

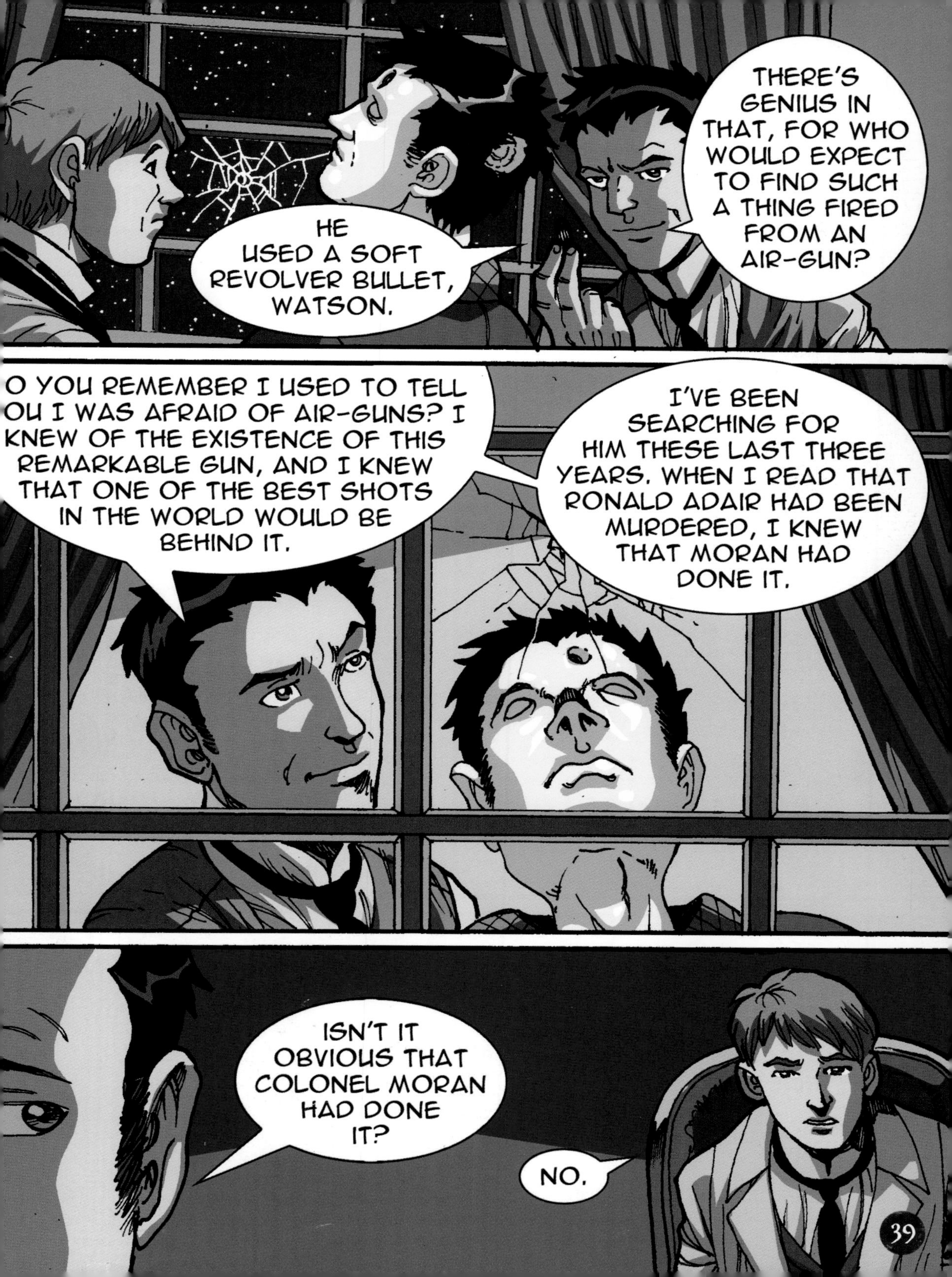
THERE'S GENIUS IN THAT, FOR WHO WOULD EXPECT TO FIND SUCH A THING FIRED FROM AN AIR-GUN?
HE USED A SOFT REVOLVER BULLET, WATSON.
O YOU REMEMBER I USED TO TELL OU I WAS AFRAID OF AIR-GUNS? I KNEW OF THE EXISTENCE OF THIS REMARKABLE GUN, AND I KNEW THAT ONE OF THE BEST SHOTS IN THE WORLD WOULD BE BEHIND IT.
I'VE BEEN SEARCHING FOR HIM THESE LAST THREE YEARS. WHEN I READ THAT RONALD ADAIR HAD BEEN MURDERED, I KNEW THAT MORAN HAD DONE IT.
ISN'T IT OBVIOUS THAT COLONEL MORAN HAD DONE IT?
NO.

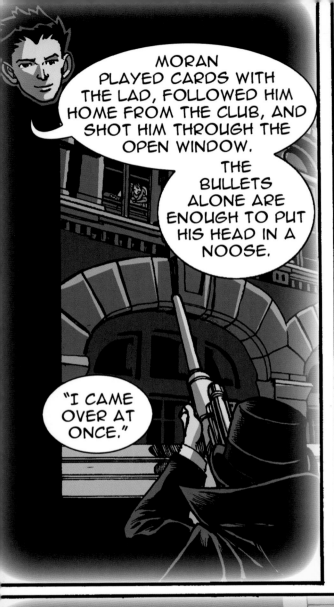

MORAN PLAYED CARDS WITH THE LAD, FOLLOWED HIM HOME FROM THE CLUB, AND SHOT HIM THROUGH THE OPEN WINDOW. THE BULLETS ALONE ARE ENOUGH TO PUT HIS HEAD IN A NOOSE.

"I CAME OVER AT ONCE."

"I WAS SEEN BY ONE OF MORAN'S MEN, WHO DIRECTED THE COLONEL'S ATTENTION TO MY PRESENCE."

"I WAS SURE THAT HE WOULD MAKE AN ATTEMPT TO GET ME OUT OF THE WAY AT ONCE AND WOULD BRING ROUND HIS MURDEROUS WEAPON FOR THAT PURPOSE."

"I LEFT HIM AN EXCELLENT MARK IN THE WINDOW AND WARNED THE POLICE THAT THEY MIGHT BE NEEDED."

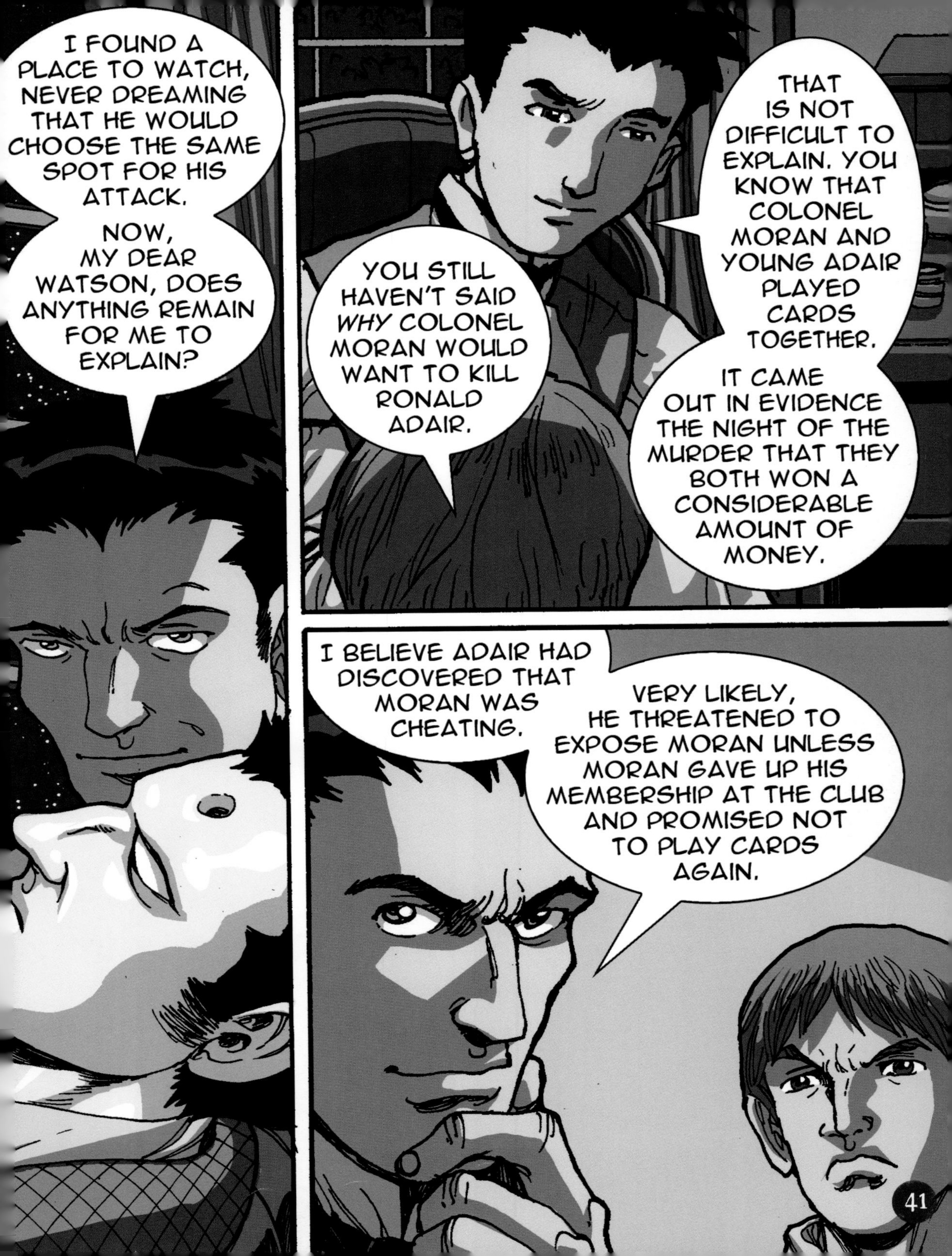
I FOUND A PLACE TO WATCH, NEVER DREAMING THAT HE WOULD CHOOSE THE SAME SPOT FOR HIS ATTACK.
NOW, MY DEAR WATSON, DOES ANYTHING REMAIN FOR ME TO EXPLAIN?
YOU STILL HAVEN'T SAID *WHY* COLONEL MORAN WOULD WANT TO KILL RONALD ADAIR.
THAT IS NOT DIFFICULT TO EXPLAIN. YOU KNOW THAT COLONEL MORAN AND YOUNG ADAIR PLAYED CARDS TOGETHER.
IT CAME OUT IN EVIDENCE THE NIGHT OF THE MURDER THAT THEY BOTH WON A CONSIDERABLE AMOUNT OF MONEY.
I BELIEVE ADAIR HAD DISCOVERED THAT MORAN WAS CHEATING.
VERY LIKELY, HE THREATENED TO EXPOSE MORAN UNLESS MORAN GAVE UP HIS MEMBERSHIP AT THE CLUB AND PROMISED NOT TO PLAY CARDS AGAIN.

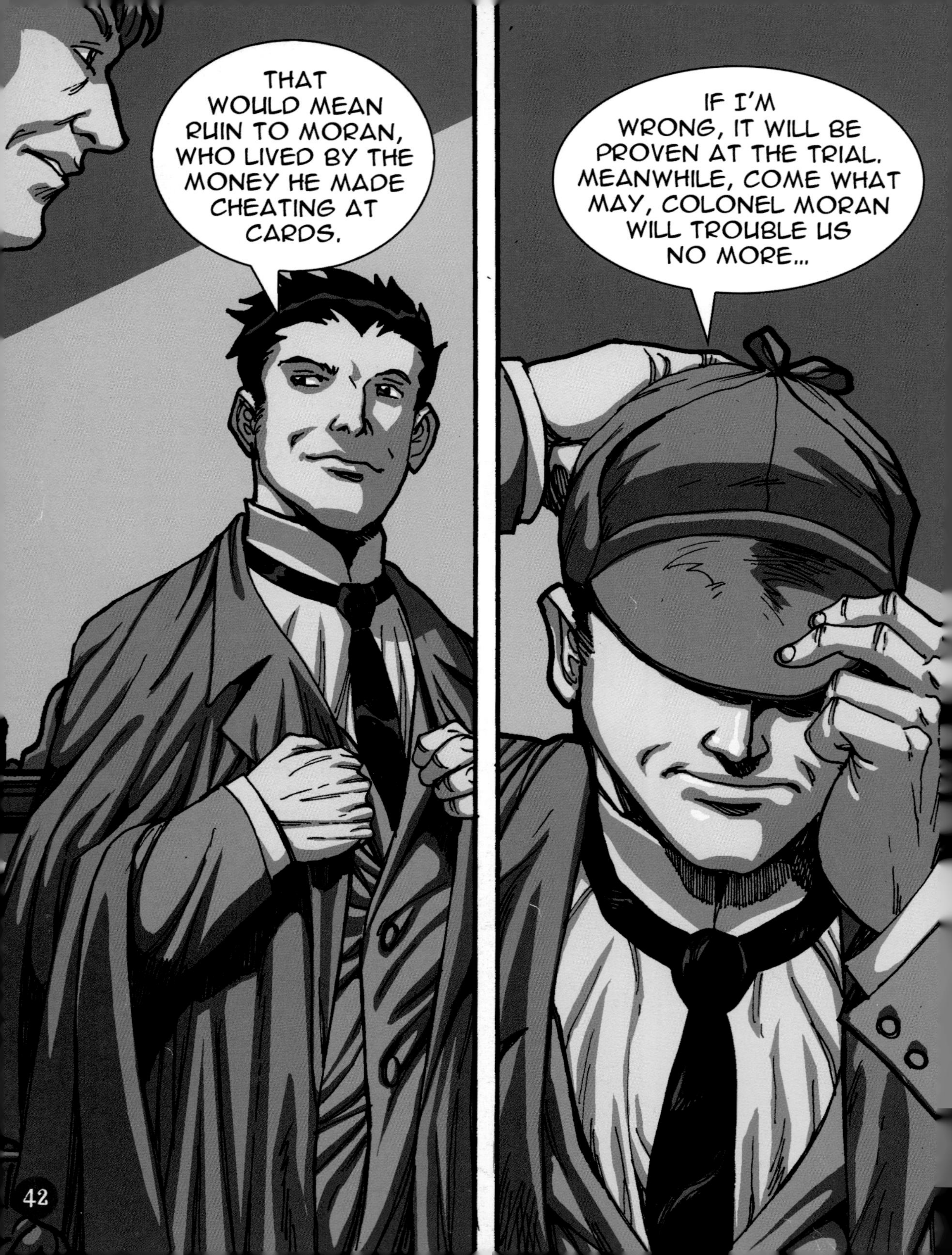
THAT WOULD MEAN RUIN TO MORAN, WHO LIVED BY THE MONEY HE MADE CHEATING AT CARDS.
IF I'M WRONG, IT WILL BE PROVEN AT THE TRIAL. MEANWHILE, COME WHAT MAY, COLONEL MORAN WILL TROUBLE US NO MORE...

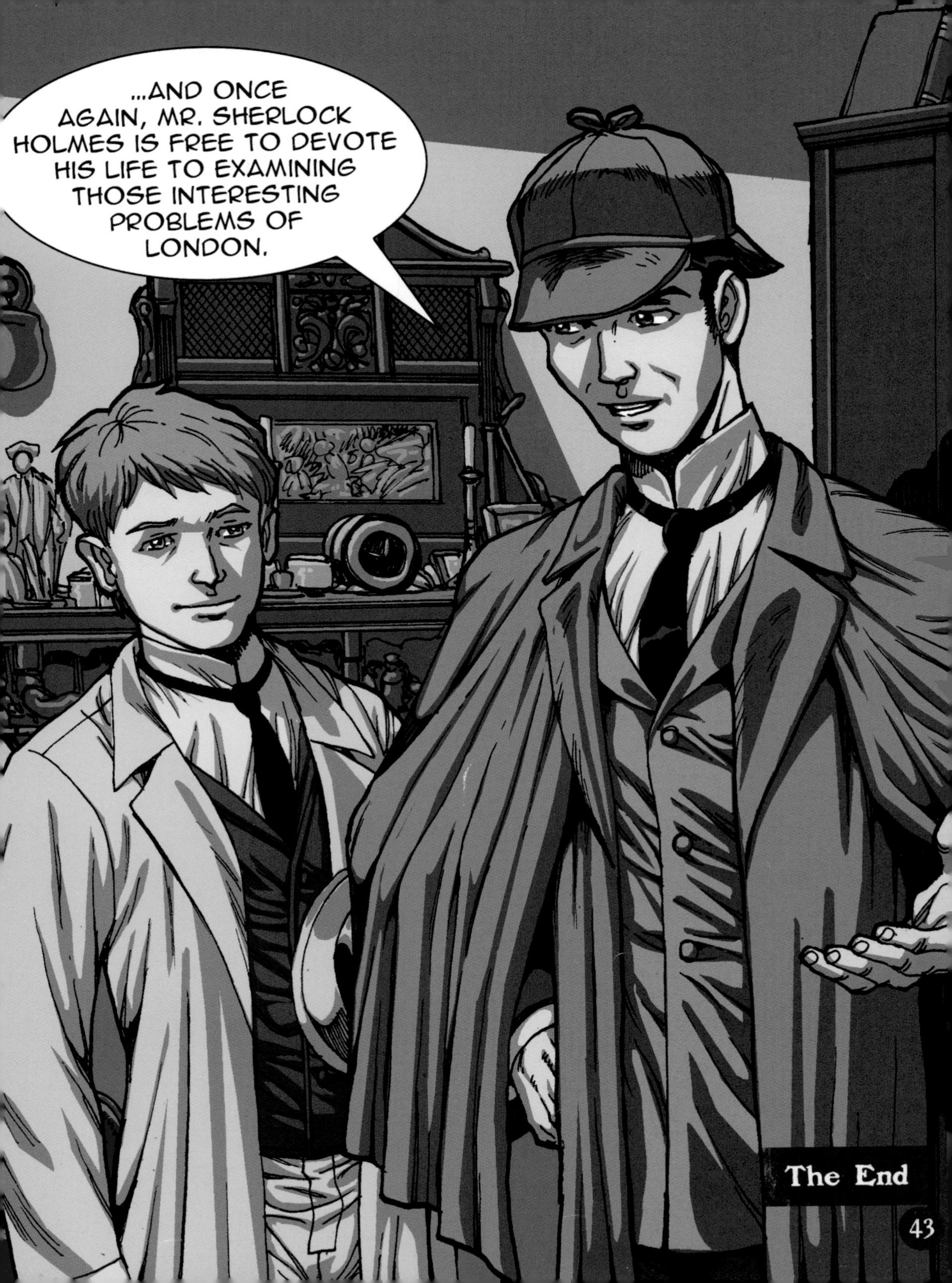
...AND ONCE AGAIN, MR. SHERLOCK HOLMES IS FREE TO DEVOTE HIS LIFE TO EXAMINING THOSE INTERESTING PROBLEMS OF LONDON.
The End

How to Draw
Sherlock Holmes

by Ben Dunn

Step 1: Use a pencil to draw a simple framework. You can start with a stick figure! Then add circles, ovals, and cylinders to get the basic form. Getting the simple shapes in place is the beginning to solving any great case.

Step 2: Time to add to Sherlock's look. Use the shapes you started with to fill in his clothes. Use guidelines to add circles for the eyes. And don't forget the hair.

Step 3: Now you can go in with a pen and start inking Sherlock. Fill in all the details and fix any mistakes. Let the ink dry to avoid smudges, then erase any pencil marks. Sherlock is ready for some color, so grab your markers and get started!

Glossary

abstract - relating to something that doesn't represent a real object but expresses ideas or emotions.

aristocrat- a person who is born into a high social class. Aristocrats run the government in some countries.

awe - an emotion of dread and wonder.

contraption - a gadget or tool.

evidence - something that provides proof of an action or crime.

foremost - the first rank.

inadequate - not good enough.

pound - an English coin equal to 12 shillings. Twelve shillings weigh one pound (.5 kg).

pursuit - the act of following someone or something.

unique - being the only one of its kind.

Web Sites

To learn more about Sir Arthur Conan Doyle, visit ABDO Group online at **www.abdopublishing.com**. Web sites about Doyle are featured on our Book Links page. These links are routinely monitored and updated to provide the most current information available.

About the Author

Arthur Conan Doyle was born on May 22, 1859, in Edinburgh, Scotland. He was the second of Charles Altamont and Mary Foley Doyle's ten children. In 1868, Conan Doyle began his schooling in England. Eight years later, he returned to Scotland.

Upon his return, Doyle entered the University of Edinburgh's medical school, where he became a doctor in 1885. That year, he married Louisa Hawkins. Together they had two children.

While a medical student, Doyle was impressed when his professor observed the tiniest details of a patient's condition. Doyle later wrote stories where his most famous character, Sherlock Holmes, used this same technique to solve mysteries. Holmes first appeared in *A Study in Scarlet* in 1887 and was immediately popular.

Between 1887 and 1927, Doyle wrote 66 stories and 3 novels about Holmes. He also wrote other fiction and nonfiction novels throughout his life. In 1902, Doyle was knighted for his work in a field hospital in the South African War. Four years later, Louisa died. Doyle married Jean Leckie in 1907, and they had three children together.

Sir Arthur Conan Doyle died on July 7, 1930, in Sussex, England. Today, Doyle's famous character, Sherlock Holmes, is honored with societies around the world that pay tribute to the detective.

Additional Works

A Study in Scarlet (1887)

The Mystery of Cloomber (1889)

The Firm of Girdlestone (1890)

The White Company (1891)

The Adventures of Sherlock Holmes (1891-92)

The Memoirs of Sherlock Holmes (1892-93)

Round the Red Lamp (1894)

The Stark Munro Letters (1895)

The Great Boer War (1900)

The Hound of the Baskervilles (1901-02)

The Return of Sherlock Holmes (1903-04)

Through the Magic Door (1907)

The Crime of the Congo (1909)

The Coming of the Fairies (1922)

Memories and Adventures (1924)

The Case-Book of Sherlock Holmes (1921-1927)

Author

Vincent Goodwin earned his B.A. in Drama and Communications from Trinity University in San Antonio. He is the writer of three plays as well as the cowriter of the comic book *Pirates vs. Ninjas II*. Goodwin is also an accomplished journalist, having won several awards for his work as a columnist and reporter.

Illustrator

Ben Dunn founded Antarctic Press, one of the largest comic companies in the United States. His works appear in Marvel and Image comics. He is best known for his series *Ninja High School* and *Warrior Nun Areala*.